GEOFFREY CHAUCER started work on *The Canterbury Tales* in about 1387. He portrayed a set of some thirty pilgrims and intended that each pilgrim should tell two stories on the way to Canterbury and two on the way back. But he never finished or revised the work and died in 1400.

He drew his stories from all over Europe, from ancient writers, and from the East. The title of each story came from the name of the pilgrim who told it, e.g. The Pardoner's Tale, and he gave most of the stories a prologue. In this version we have chosen a title that reflects the story rather than the teller. The prologues become the pilgrims' conversations with each other before a new story is started. Chaucer wrote the stories in Middle English in rhyming verse. The first two lines in the original sound like this:

> Whan that Aprille with his shoures soote
> The droghte of March hath perced to the roote…

The Canterbury Tales

Geraldine McCaughrean

Illustrated by
Victor G Ambrus

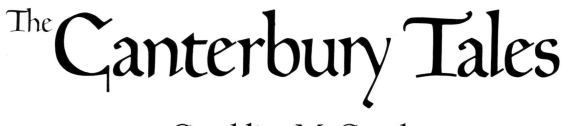

Oxford University Press

Contents

Prologue

APRIL rain was dripping off the branches as I rode beneath them. But the last sunlight of a fine spring day made the leaves shine, and I was glad to be on my way. I could stay the night at the Tabard Inn in Southwark, then make a start for Canterbury by first light.

But it seemed I was not the only one on the Kent road that day. As I stabled my horse, I found twenty other animals, their heads already in the manger, rending noisily at the knots of hay. Their saddles were hung up above their stalls. And as I opened the low door and ducked into the Tabard's yellow warmth, my eyes stung and my nose filled with the reek of cooking and wood smoke.

'Geoffrey!' roared the innkeeper, pushing his way between two priests to greet me at the door.

No one makes you more welcome than my good friend Harry Bailey, innkeeper of the Tabard. He can remember a guest's name from one year to the next, and he's always ready with a hot meal and a jug of the finest. I do believe he keeps the best inn south of the river.

'You'll have good company for your pilgrimage this year, friend,' he said, beaming at me. 'There must be a dozen other pilgrims in already.'

'It's the time of the year,' said a grey-headed knight sitting close by. 'The spring comes round clean and fresh, and people want to put themselves right with God. Besides, the winter roads haven't been passable until now. I'm just back from Normandy, and my horse was forever knee-deep in mud over there.'

I liked him at once, this quiet, noble-looking man. From the mud on his jerkin, he looked as if he had travelled half Christendom, and I thought he might have a few good tales to tell. So I sat down beside him and looked around at my fellow pilgrims.

What a gallery of faces! They were about as many as the letters of the alphabet – and each one equally different from his neighbour.

There were priests and nuns and tradesmen; men down from the city and up from the country; guildsmen and labourers. A gawky scholar sat in a corner reading, while a gigantic woman in an enormous hat sat on the other end of his bench shouting and laughing in a voice that drowned most others.

'Do you know any of these people?' I asked the knight.

'The lad over there is my son. You see? The one playing the lute and singing to the barmaid. He wrote the song himself.' (I picked him out – a handsome, curly-haired boy in an embroidered shirt.) 'And the yeoman in the green coat, he's my boy's serving-man.'

The door beside me opened, and a smell of onions burst in, closely followed by a fright of a man. His face was covered in boils and spots and weeping sores. I swear, even his sweat smelt of pickled onions—and his sweat had been with him for a *long* time. Yet another Christian was making his yearly pilgrimage.

For the rest of the evening, pilgrims straggled into the Tabard and paid for a meal, a blanket and a cup or two of mulled wine. By eight o'clock there were thirty of us, all bound for Canterbury. Cattle-drovers travelling up from the Old Kent Road put their heads round the door, saw the crowd, and went back to sleep with their cows. My friend the innkeeper was enjoying excellent business, and it put him in a particularly agreeable mood. I was just thinking of going to bed when he banged down his mug on a table and called out:

'Listen here, friends! You'll all ride as a party tomorrow, won't you?'

'Only sensible,' said a brusque, quick-eyed fellow. 'Footpads. Highwaymen. Kent. Notorious. Only sensible.'

'Well, I've a mind to go with you,' said Harry Bailey. 'But I know that ride. It's a long time to sit in a hard saddle. Let's liven up the journey with a competition. Each of us can tell a story, and whoever tells the best will get a free dinner on the way back. The rest of us will foot the bill.'

'Yes! Yes!' Most of us cheered and stamped our feet (although the Scholar in the corner went on reading his book, hearing nothing).

'I'll be the judge. And the judge's word is final!' Harry declared, grinning broadly.

'Ah . . . er . . . well, perhaps a vote . . .' said a pale-eyed man with a few strands of blond wispy hair. But our host cut him off short:

'And anyone who quarrels with my rules pays the expenses of the entire trip!'

'Yes! Done! Agreed! Settled!' The blond man was silenced by more stamping and clapping and cheering as the warm wine settled comfortably on our stomachs, and we all began to feel like life-long companions. Some clergyman pointed out that Saint Paul called story-telling an unholy waste of time, but we managed to ignore him.

Quite soon, the wine settled heavily on our eyelids, too, and one by one we went upstairs to the rickety cribs of the Tabard's dormitory. I lay down and began racking my brains for a story to tell. My Canterbury pilgrimage promised to be more entertaining than usual.

I wouldn't like you to think that I was looking forward more to the stories than to visiting the shrine of holy Saint Thomas. But there's more to be said for pilgrimages than just seeing a holy place.

You often meet such extraordinary people on the way.

NEXT morning, we were stumbling about the yard in the cold and dark, in a welter of horses and a net of rain. A shape I had mistaken for the gate post and who proved to be the Miller, cursed the weather and wished himself home in bed.

''Tis nought but God's holy water to bless us on our way,' said the gentle voice of the Ploughman, as he packed straw under his saddle in place of a rug.

I began to work out who everybody was and which of the pilgrims were travelling together. The Parson who disapproved of stories was the Ploughman's brother. The noisy, evil-smelling individual with the horrible face was also a religious gentleman – a Summoner – travelling with a pale, giggling Pardoner who had long, sparse, blond hair. I had to look twice to see it was not a woman.

4

The biggest party was made up of master-craftsmen.
Suspicious of Kent's inns, they had even brought along their
own Cook – a man stuffed as full of recipes as a sucking-pig with
apples. To hear him talk made your mouth water. If he had just
stopped drinking, and picking that sore on his leg, I might have
employed him myself.

From the tangle of reins, I sorted out my own, mounted, dismounted,
told the Ship's Captain he was on my horse, and helped him on to his.
Very soon, like a row of chessmen escaping from the chessboard, we
ambled off the paved yard and into the quagmire of the drover's road.

5

Gradually, as the light strengthened, I could make out the different colours of clothes, the different quality of the horses, the pale, bleary faces of the silent riders. Beside me the Knight's chain mail began to shine like fishes' scales in the half light.

Suddenly, through the mist loomed a horrible sight. A massive, dark shape, bristling all over with long, curved spines, was shuffling towards us enveloped in a smell as thick as fog. I reined in.

The Knight beside me gave a great round laugh that set his chain shirt clanking. 'You city people! Anyone would think you'd never seen a herd of cows before!'

Then a steer raised its curved horns and bellowed. The drovers with their long whips emerged from the mist, and the herd swept past and between us as if we were ghosts.

'I was all set to run home and hide under the bed,' I admitted, laughing shamefacedly. 'I'm no Saint George when it comes to fighting dragons. I never could see the point in gallantry . . . oh.'

I could have kicked myself. The Knight had spent most of his life fighting in one war or another. But he smiled generously and said: 'I agree, Master Chaucer. There's far too much unnecessary killing nowadays among these "fashionable" young knights. Life's too precious. Fights to the death ought to be over matters of life and death, that's my opinion. I never had much time for Palamon and Arcite.'

'Who?'

Then Harry interrupted. He was holding out a bundle of straws to each rider, saying: 'Take one, take a straw.'

'What's this for?' I asked, pulling out a long straw.

'You're all so modest. I can't get anyone to tell the first story! So we're drawing straws. The person who draws the short straw tells the first story.'

'Oh dear,' said the Knight, holding up the short straw. 'I'm not sure I know any stories.' His face began to redden with shyness as the riders surrounded him, gaped at him expectantly.

'What about Palamon and Arcite?' I suggested.

'Ah yes. Just so. Right.' He cleared his throat, looked around him with a plea for patience, and began – the first unwilling entrant in our competition.

6

Chivalry and Rivalry

BELOW the smoking walls of Thebes, two thousand men grappled, sword to sword and hand to hand. The battle between the forces of King Creon and the troops of Duke Theseus was long, fierce and bloody. And when it was over – when Creon's army had been put to flight – the ground was carpeted with fallen knights.

Athenian soldiers, searching the battlefield for their own wounded companions, found two young knights lying side by side. But as they stepped across the two bodies, one stirred, groaned, and opened his eyes. 'Arcite! Cousin! Where are you?' he whispered.

His companion was not dead, either. Both were carried as prisoners to the tent of Duke Theseus. 'Take them to Athens, and lock them in the prison-tower of my palace,' said the Duke.

Despite the cold stones and hard floor of their tower-top prison, both Arcite and his cousin Palamon gradually recovered from their wounds. Their devoted friendship made the passing days, weeks and months bearable, though both grew dreadfully bored.

The narrow arrow slit, which let in the only sunlight they ever saw, overlooked the Duke's garden. Each day they would take it in turns to balance on a stool and gaze down at the flowers, and at the gardener pruning the rose trees.

One day there was a new visitor to the garden. Palamon was balancing on the stool at the time, and his feet slipped and almost tipped it over. 'Oh Arcite!' he exclaimed. 'I never realized until this moment why I was born. Now I've seen her. She is the reason! Zeus! She can't be flesh and blood. She must be an angel!'

'Come down. It's my turn for the stool,' said Arcite, and he took Palamon's place.

Down in the garden, Duke Theseus' young sister-in-law, Emily, had come to gather flowers in a wicker basket. She sang as she picked them – and the flowers seemed to turn up their faces towards her, and to faint at the touch of her hand.

'Oh lady! I'll wear your favour until the day I die!' said Arcite breathlessly to himself.

Palamon pulled the stool away, and they both fell in a heap to the floor. 'What? Are you making fun of me, Arcite? It's serious! I'm in love with her!'

'You? You didn't even think she was human! It's I who love her.'

'You Judas! You cuckoo! Where are your vows of lifelong friendship now? The first chance you get, you stab me in the back. You . . . you . . .'

'Viper! You thieving magpie!'

This undignified scene was interrupted by the gaoler bringing in their one frugal meal of the day. 'What's this, puppies?' he said setting down the tray. 'Is this cell getting too small for the two of you? Well I've got news for whichever one of you is Sir Arcite. Sir Arcite has a friend in Athens, it would appear. And this friend has spoken to Duke Theseus, and won your freedom. You can leave tomorrow.'

Arcite stared. Palamon got to his feet. 'Cousin!' he said. 'In all our lives, we have never been parted! Is there no message for *me*, gaoler? Has no one asked for *my* freedom?'

'No. You stay. And you, Sir Arcite, must be out of this land by sunset tomorrow. On pain of death are you forbidden to return.'

'Leave the country? Leave Athens? But I don't *want* to go!' protested Arcite. 'You go instead of me, Palamon. If I'm banished from Athens, I'll never see *her* again!'

Perhaps he saw, or perhaps he imagined a smile playing on Palamon's lips. Anyway, the two cousins, who all life long had been inseparable, barely spoke during that last night in the tower.

Next week, Palamon was still a captive, balancing all day on the stool to watch for Emily. Far away, his cousin sat in his own house, the windows and doors all shut as if it were a prison – for he was pining for Emily.

'Which do you think was better off?' mused the Knight, thoughtlessly interrupting his own story. 'Was it the man in prison or the man in exile?'

'Lord love you, have you no spark of wit?' demanded the lady I recognized from the night before by the enormous size of her hat. 'If the boy in exile had one half a brain, he'd disguise himself and go back to

9

Athens. If all he can do is sit around and mope, he doesn't *deserve* the woman!'

'Well, well,' said the Knight, rather taken aback by the strength of her feelings. 'That's just what happened.'

Arcite grew a beard, dressed as an Athenian, and took work as a servant in the very house where Emily lived. The thought of seeing her again quite outweighed the threat of death if he was discovered inside Athens.

Every day he saw her. Every day he took orders from her lips. Every day he was able to reach out and touch the chair where she had sat, the glass from which she had drunk. He thought he would be happy for ever.

He was happy for just a week. Then the questions began to creep into his mind. 'What good is this? How is this better than being in prison? How can a "servant" speak of love to the sister-in-law of Duke Theseus?' So he fell to brooding, to chewing his pillow at night, and cursing the hour he was born.

Just two hours after the gaoler forgot to lock the door of the prison tower, Palamon found himself free, creeping through the Athenian woods, his heart in his mouth, his life in the balance. 'Now's my only chance,' he thought. 'I'll find the lady Emily and ravish her away to my own country.'

A rustling of leaves sent him bolting like a rabbit into the bowl of a hollow tree. He squatted down low, despising his thumping heart, and despising his fate for bringing an honourable knight to such a pass.

The approaching footsteps halted beside the tree, and Palamon held his breath. Surely the Duke's men were not searching for him yet? Peeping through a knothole, he could see a man sitting dejectedly among the spreading roots, throwing pebbles at his own boots. 'What's the use?' he was muttering. 'I might just as well be rotting in prison with Palamon.'

'You asp! You wolf-in-sheep's clothing!' Palamon flung himself out of the tree and grabbed Arcite by his beard. 'What are you doing, sneaking back here to prowl round my Emily?'

'Don't you talk about my mistress and lady like that, you convict, you escaped prisoner!'

'I'm an honourable knight!' Palamon maintained, despite the hammer-blows Arcite was raining on his head. 'I love Emily far more than you do!'

'Heartsblood! Death's too good for you, you traitor to all things honourable!'

'Goat!'

'Skunk!'

'Rat!'

As they pranced, grunting through the trees, their arms locked fast round one another, a wolfhound came barking round their legs excitedly. Then there was another – and another – and another – until the clearing was awash with dogs. Into the mêlée burst a hunting party on horseback, and at its head Duke Theseus himself.

'Part those men and bring them here! One of them is Emily's serving-man. The other looks like one of Creon's men!'

'He is! He's an escaped convict!' Arcite shouted.

'And he's Arcite – banished on pain of death!' called Palamon. 'You see, cousin? I can play as dirty as you!'

Theseus laughed in disbelief. 'Is this the devoted twosome we took prisoner at Thebes? Bosom friends never to be parted? In the name of all that's friendly, what's this quarrel about?'

Arcite and Palamon wiped their muddy faces, and rubbed their bruised eyes. Then both together they said: 'HER!'

Emily had come riding into the clearing on a white mare. She wore a blue mantle, and even the hounds fell back whimpering at the sight of her.

11

Arcite sprang to one stirrup, Palamon to the other. 'Lady, your eye has scorched me like a burning-glass!'

'Emily! Your name is a millstone crushing my heart!'

'Sweetheart, if I were to live two hundred . . .'

'Enough!' roared Theseus. 'What is this competition of compliments? If you're going to compete, at least do it the man's way! Tomorrow I'm holding a joust. Both your lives are forfeit, but I shall spare the man who remains alive when the joust ends. Prepare yourselves – for tomorrow you fight in the lists!'

Not until sundown, when they were billetted in separate tents on the field of combat, did Palamon and Arcite stop quarrelling. Outside Arcite's tent, an armourer was sharpening a sword with a stone. It grated and screeched. A chill went through the knight, but he called to mind Emily's radiant face, and went happily to sleep. Outside Palamon's tent, a squire was sharpening his master's lance with a knife. The shavings fell on to the canopy and made shadows like a swarm of spiders. A chill went through Palamon, but he thought of Emily, and how pleased she would be by his chivalrous heroism, and he went to sleep contented.

The joust was a circus of colour. Knights caparisoned in mail, heraldic surcoats, and plumes fit for birds-of-paradise were brazed by the blaring of trumpets whose scarlet oriflammes were embroidered with silvery beasts. Blade by blade, the grass was turfed out in divots by the flying hooves of horses. The pavilions flapped like Chinese kites. By midday, the ladies tripping back and forth to their seats had scarlet hems where their gowns had swept the field.

In the hottest part of the day, Arcite and Palamon found themselves at opposite ends of the jousting fence. Palamon's lance weighed heavy in the crook of his arm after so many months in prison. The squires blew a shrill fanfare. The horses rattled the bits between their teeth and pranced towards one another.

On the first pass, both lances missed their mark, and the two cousins passed shoulder to shoulder, grimacing into one another's face.

On the second pass, Palamon saw the point of Arcite's lance bearing squarely for his chest. He flung himself forward along his horse's neck, dropping his own lance. But the oncoming lance-tip tore through the back of his tunic, caught in his belt, and lifted him out of the saddle, pitching him to the ground. Arcite's lance was dragged from his grip, but he turned at the head of the lists and came galloping back down the field, swinging his mace.

Its iron spikes bruised the air with each whistling circle the mace-head made on its chain stalk. Palamon, his head uncovered, fell to

his knees, but he knew he could not escape the swinging iron. In the grass, his hands brushed the lance that had dragged him from his horse. His fingers closed round its haft, and he was lifting it to protect himself, when Arcite, stretching from his saddle to strike the mortal blow, rode straight on to its point.

His face cleared of all expression. His horse rode from under him, and he stood for a moment with the lance planted in his chest. The mace dropped from his hand, and he spread his fingers across the red of his surcoat. 'Cousin,' he said, then fell dead on his back, the lance rising like a mast out of his hull.

Palamon took off his gauntlets and crawled across the grass to

Arcite's side. 'Friend,' he said, touching his cousin's cheek. 'What have we done?'

Then the crowds were upon him, praising, congratulating. Duke Theseus was there, and Emily too, though Palamon could not recognize her at first among the other women. They were all quite pretty . . .

Theseus began: 'Arcite, my boy . . .'

'Palamon. I'm Palamon.'

'Oh. Well, Palamon, my boy, let this be an end to all quarrelling. Your rival has died a glorious death in the name of chivalry. And you have fought bravely, too. Take Emily's hand, and forget every unhappiness. The wedding shall be tomorrow!'

Hanging back in the shadow of her brother-in-law, Emily said: 'Urgh, do I have to? His hair's awfully thin already, and I don't like his mouth.' She had a voice like the teeth of a comb clicking.

'Nonsense, Emily. He's a very chivalrous knight – even if he is a foreigner. Emily – Arcite: my blessing on you both!'

'Palamon. I'm Palamon,' said the chivalrous knight, while at his feet Arcite raised no argument, no argument whatsoever.

The Knight stopped speaking. The woman in the enormous hat (who I learned was a widow all the way from Bath) had been leaning out of her saddle to catch the Knight's words. She was rather deaf, I think. She continued leaning towards him, waiting for more. 'Well?' she demanded in a huge, West Country voice. 'Were they happy?'

The Knight shook himself. 'Yes, oh yes. They both lived happily ever after. Palamon woke to each day happier than the day before.' The Widow smiled and sat back into her saddle with a thump.

'I don't know if he would – under the circumstances,' I said.

'Under *these* circumstances,' said the Knight, waving a hand towards the listening pilgrims, 'we had to have a happy ending. Now who's next?'

'All the same,' said a pebble-headed Reeve snarlingly, 'it wasn't a whole heap of laughs, your story.'

The Knight freely admitted it. 'I'm afraid I couldn't think of a *funny* story, off-hand.'

'Well I can,' said the Reeve. We seemed to be about to hear his story, whether we liked it or not.

W HO asked you?' Red as a firebrand, the Miller's hair and beard showed through the mist like beacons. With flaring black nostrils housed in a red, tufted nose, the Miller rampaged down on us like a wild boar. The Reeve's fingers closed round the handle of the carpenter's mallet but he did not pull it from his saddle bag. 'Drunk already, Matt?' he said, blipping the Miller's horse on the nose with his reins as it cannoned into him.

'What if I am, you woodpecker?' retorted the Miller. 'Isn't it bad enough to be traipsing through fog and rain and up to our noses in mud . . .'

'Best place for your nose,' muttered the Reeve.

'Isn't it bad enough, without having to listen to a chiselling carpenter?'

'Hey! Hey! What is this between you?' said Harry. 'Have you two brought some old grudge along with you?'

Oswald the Reeve did not so much answer as growl in the general direction of Matt. 'Just because I do him a favour – knock him up a lean-to for his mill – and at a price he wouldn't get from any carpenter in the South of England – these are the thanks I get!'

'The wood was so rotten it fell in on my head the first time I so much as touched it!'

'At the price you paid, what do you expect – mahogany?'

'Whoa there!' Harry protested. 'Let's have a story, not a war!'

But the Reeve was sulking by this time. Or perhaps he rode off to the back of the line to be a safe distance from the Miller's swinging fists. I swear, Arcite's iron mace swinging down on Palamon's head couldn't have done more damage than those fists on the end of those arms!

The moment the Reeve was out of sound and sight, Matt the Miller cheered up hugely. He got out his bagpipes and struck up a tune – so hideously strident, so tunelessly discordant, that we begged him to stop and tell us a story instead.

'I hoped you might say that,' he said, and the drone of his pipes died away like an expiring sheep. 'Down at Osney Mead in Oxford . . .'

The Scholar, an Oxford man himself, looked up from the book he was reading. 'I'm acquainted with it,' he said.

'What?' snarled the Miller. 'You mean you've heard my story before?'

'No. I simply observed that I know Osney Mead.'

'Ah. That's all right, then. No more butting in, though – right?' The Scholar gave a bewildered shrug, and went back to his book. The Miller glared round at us, then his ruined face collapsed into a grin that showed all his tombstone teeth. 'I have to admit – I'm a bit tipsy: I can tell from the way my words are coming out. If you have any trouble following, just shout. And ladies . . . if I give offence, blame it on the drink!'

I'm not sure I ought to relay the story with which Matt the Miller regaled us. It wasn't – how shall I say? – it wasn't the kind of story you hear in church or recount to your mother when you get home. Still, it fetched a lot of laughter from some of the pilgrims, so I had best not keep it from you.

If you find it a little *rude*, you had better cover your eyes while you read.

A Barrel of Laughs

DOWN at Osney Mead in Oxford lived a carpenter called Oswald – a crusty old misery – just like him over there. But he had married a pretty young thing called Alison.

Now *everyone* was in love with Alison. She was as pert and as pretty as a squirrel up a tree, though to tell the truth, she should not have flirted so much with the men. Most of the time she was only joking – like with poor Absalom, the clerk. But Absalom got quite the wrong idea. He was all set to elope with her whenever she said the word.

Nicholas was a different pot of jam.

Nicholas was a lodger in the Carpenter's house. And Alison just could not take her eyes off him. He was allowed to steal a kiss in the dark of the larder and while he helped her hang out the washing.

The Carpenter, knowing he wasn't the prettiest duck on the pond, was fearfully jealous about his pretty young wife. He never let her go out alone, and trusted her in the company of no man – except Nicholas.

'Nicholas is an *educated* man,' he would tell his neighbours proudly, 'a clever man, a *religious* man.'

It was true that Nicholas was clever. It was *he* who thought up the plot, after all – a plot to make an utter fool of the Carpenter. He whispered the plot to Alison who giggled behind her hand. Then he went to his room with food enough for a fortnight, and locked himself in.

'Where's Nicholas?' said the Carpenter three days later. 'He hasn't eaten with us since Monday.'

Then Alison wrung her hands. 'I'm worried about him, husband. He locked himself in his room on Monday with nothing to eat. He won't answer to knocking. He must be ill. But what can I do?'

'Well, why didn't you say so, woman?' The Carpenter leapt up the stairs and hammered on the lodger's door. 'Nicholas! Nicholas, old son! Open up, won't you?' And when he got no answer, he threw himself against the door until it fell off its hinges.

There sat Nicholas, bolt upright, on the edge of his bed. His eyes were lifted towards the ceiling, and a strange humming came from his nose.

'Lord have mercy! I told you he was religious,' cried Oswald. 'He's in some kind of trance. He's seeing visions!' And shaking Nicholas by the hair, he shouted in his ear: 'Wake up, boy! Snap out of it!'

One blink, two blinks, and Nicholas closed his mouth with a sigh. 'Ah, brother Oswald, I've been visited by the angels and they showed me such visions!'

'What? Tell us – what?'

Then Nicholas clapped the Carpenter in an embrace and said tearfully: 'You've been like a father to me. So I'm going to tell you a terrible secret. The angels themselves revealed it to me. The End of the World is coming!'

'Jesus, Mary, and Joseph,' said the Carpenter crossing himself. 'What – fire and brimstone?'

'No, no,' said Nicholas in the most saintly of voices. 'You remember Noah?'

'Well of *course* I remember Noah,' Oswald burst out excitedly. 'Noah who?'

Nicholas sighed, with all the patience of a holy martyr. 'You remember how in the Bible we are told that God sent rain for forty days and forty nights and the whole world was drowned – except for Noah who built an ark, that's to say, a boat. And he floated to safety and started up the human race all over again after the Flood dried up.'

'Is it rain, then? Are we all to be drowned, me and you and little Alison and the cat . . .'

'All, all' said Nicholas in sepulchral tones. 'Unless . . .'

He told the Carpenter to fetch three big, watertight barrels, and to hang them up among the roof beams of the house by stout hemp ropes – a barrel for each of them. 'When the rains come, the flood will rise and rise until it sets the barrels afloat. Then, at a given signal, we shall cut the ropes and float away on the tide. Take a bite of bread and cheese up there with you. We may be floating about for some time before God ends the Flood.'

Calling down blessings from Heaven on Nicholas, the Carpenter hung the three barrels in the roof, climbed into one, and sat waiting for the Flood. When, after an hour or so, it got boring waiting for the Flood, he dozed off and dreamt he was ruling the empty world with Alison on one side of his throne and Nicholas on the other.

Down below, Nicholas and Alison fell into each other's arms in fits of helpless, silent laughter. They sat on the settle and held hands and kissed and carried on until the darkest hours of the night, when the whole town else was asleep.

A sudden soft tapping on the shutters made them both sit up with a start. It was followed by a quiet, high-pitched 'Cooo'.

'Alison! It's me!'

'It's Absalom!'

'Alison! Sugar pie! Honey bee! Baby bubbles! Chick-a-dee! Give me a kiss, won't you? Everyone's asleep but you and me. Even the moon's hiding herself tonight. Now we can steal a kiss, can't we?'

Alison clapped her hand over her mouth, then whispered: 'What shall I do, Nicholas? He'll wake Oswald.'

Sure enough, a bleary voice from overhead said: 'Has the Flood come? Is it time yet?'

'No, dear. Go back to sleep,' called Alison, and soon snores were rending the rafters like a bow saw. But still Absalom was at the window. 'What shall I do?' hissed Alison.

'I suppose he must have his kiss,' said Nicholas rising from the settle. The window was high up, higher than a man's head. In a voice as high as a filleted cod, Nicholas whispered through the shutter: 'Dearest boy. How I've longed for this moment! But close your eyes. It's not fitting that a woman should be seen in her nightclothes, even on the darkest of nights, and even by one she loves so dearly!' And he leaned out of the window to plant a kiss on Absalom's waiting lips.

Alison burst into such a fit of giggles that she had to stuff her apron into her mouth, and still the laughter snorted and snuffled in her nose.

Down in the street, Absalom heard the giggle, felt the Nicholas's beard tickle his chin, and guessed at the truth. He danced off down the road with such a heat of temper that his vest all but scorched. But not one sound escaped his lips – only silent, wicked curses.

Nicholas gave that little snigger of his, and they returned to the settle to complete unfinished business . . .

Tap, tap, tap. Absalom was back again. 'Alison! Dearest! That one kiss has fired such love in me that I shan't sleep a wink without you kiss me again!'

'Oh make him be quiet, Nicholas!' hissed Alison, and Nicholas smirked. Going to the window, he called through the shutters: 'This must be the last, dear heart. Now close your eyes, won't you? You may kiss me now.' And edging on to the window sill, he proffered Absalom the seat of his pants.

Absalom was waiting for him.

He had been to the forge, and heated a branding iron in the blacksmith's fire. Now he stood brandishing it like the Devil with his pitchfork. And as Nicholas' trousers came through the window, Absalom lunged!

They heard the scream in Banbury.

Up in his barrel, the Carpenter woke to hear a noise very like the end of the world, and Nicholas's voice yelling, 'Water! WATER!' as he galloped round the room and fell over the settle.

24

'It's come! The rains have come!' thought Oswald, and cut through the ropes tying his barrel to the roof – thinking to float away.

He dropped like a stone – right on top of the settle, his wife, and the lodger. The cat (who had been sleeping in Oswald's lap) gave a yowl and leapt out of the window. It found the street full of neighbours tumbling out of their beds and out of their doors to find the cause of the commotion.

The neighbours found Oswald, Nicholas and Alison, the settle, a barrel, and a plentiful supply of bread and cheese, all squandered in a heap. The Carpenter was shrieking, 'It's the end of the world! Swim for your lives!' A trickle of smoke was still rising from the seat of the lodger's trousers.

Who said what, and whether they were believed, I shan't ever know, for at this point the Reeve came back, with a tongue like a fly-swat, and demanded that the Miller be disqualified from the competition. 'He only told that story to spite me! I'm a carpenter, aren't I? I'm called Oswald, aren't I?' I thought he was going to chew the ears off his horse, he looked so aggrieved.

Then the Prioress Eglantine chimed in: 'Ooh! You've made me blush, Master Miller. *Regardez, messieurs, je suis blushing!*' she exclaimed, fanning her snow-white cheeks. 'By Saint Loy! What a coarse story!' She adjusted her wimple so that it sat well back on her forehead. 'What we really want,' she said coyly, 'is a *nice* story about *nice* people. No one will mind me saying so, but if we start having stories about *lower class* people, we're bound to end up with nasty stories like that. We want a finer sort of story altogether – glowing phrases, uplifting thoughts. I'm sure there's someone here who can tell us a story in the *grand style.*'

The Miller scowled at her. 'Lower class of people, indeed! I suppose you want stuff about princesses and heroic princes galloping about on chargers spouting bits of Latin.'

Prioress Eglantine sniffed. 'Fancy *you* knowing about Romantic Literature – a man of *your* low breeding.'

THE lap dog sprawled across the pommel of the Prioress's saddle began to wriggle and whine. Perhaps it could sense the feelings of Matt and the other working men towards its mistress. 'Dere, dere, little fellow,' lisped the nun. 'Has de nasty, coarse man upset you?'

Brother John, the priest accompanying the Prioress, rode his horse into the centre of the group and tried to take the sting out of the quarrel. 'I wonder why poets do always write about princes and princesses,' he said, as if he was thinking aloud. 'I vouch I could tell a story in the grand style about the most ordinary folk.'

Eglantine looked annoyed. '*Mon cher* John, do we have to have another story about squalid, working people?'

The Miller and his cronies growled menacingly. Brother John was unperturbed. 'I'll go one better,' he offered. 'I'll tell you a story about a couple of common chickens. And you just see if it doesn't have all the romance of *Venus and Adonis* and all the excitement of Homer's *Odyssey*.'

Eglantine primped herself in the saddle and, getting out a small mirror, examined her face intently. A strand of hair had escaped her wimple. She curled it round one finger, and it looked most fetching coiled beneath her cheek bone. 'Oh, all right, John dear. But do make it poetical. You know how *sensitive* I am.'

So John began: 'There was once a small house miles from town. Its one room was dark with soot . . .'

'Excuse me,' said the Oxford Scholar, 'but that doesn't sound like grand poetical English to me. All the words are so short.'

'*John*,' snarled Prioresss Eglantine. 'This had better be poetical . . .'

'Please don't distress yourself, lady – sir,' said Brother John, patting down their anxieties with large white hands. 'I'm saving the poetry for the hero and heroine.'

Nightmare Beast of the Firebrand Tail

THERE was once a small house miles from town. Its one room was dark with soot from the fire, and it let in no light. The wife who lived there was poor and led a plain life with her two young girls. There was milk and cheese and bread to eat, but no rich food or wines. Their clothes were drab and they had to work hard all day. But they kept fit that way, and slept well.

In the yard were three big pigs, three cows and a sheep. Oh, and there was an old cockerel, too.

Now listen and lend an ear to a story of heroism and scholarly wisdom set within the pallisade of that farmyard's fence! Hear now, and give ear, as I describe the magnificence of the aforesaid cockerel.

Crowned at birth with the name of Chanticleer, no cockerel in all the land could crow more gloriously. His head was emblazoned with a

28

comb-crest as scarlet as deep-sea coral, crenellated like the battlements of a castle wall. His beak gleamed like blackest jet, and his legs and feet were of a blue to equal the blue ceiling of the world, with cloud pennants of white as his claws. Mantling his noble shoulders was a cloak of plumes the colour of burnished gold.

This paragon of cockerels had a harem of seven lovely wives, each of their gowns tinted with the same sublime gold. But the fairest by far – whose throat was mottled with the very colours of beauty – was Madam Pertelote.

Was there ever such a charming, witty, courteous, cultured companion than this gracious bird? Chanticleer loved Madam Pertelote with a passionate tenderness, and together they sang love duets. If you have ever heard the voices of a cock and a hen, I daresay you can imagine just how sweetly those two sang!

But one early morning, Chanticleer woke, fear clutching at his noble heart. 'O woe!' he cried. 'Such a terrible dream!' (He woke Madam Pertelote with his shouting.) 'I dreamed I was in the terraced gardens of this palace of ours. I was strolling between the ornamental lake and the maze, taking the air and viewing our estates. Suddenly a ferocious beast sprang at me. It was like a dog, but with a reddish coat and a pointed nose, and black tips to his ears, and a tail like a firebrand. Oh those teeth – those blazing eyes from the very realms of hell!'

29

'Bck bck bck. What nonsense is this!' cried the fair damsel. 'You – a coward? You – afraid of a bad dream? How can I love such a chicken-livered lover? Women need their husbands to be courageous – level-headed. Anyone would think you were a common, uneducated cockerel. Remember what the Roman philosopher Cato wrote: "Pay no heed to dreams!" You know your trouble, don't you? You ate too much dinner last night. I'll mix up a laxative for you with my own fair wing.'

'O bird of birds! Hen of my heart!' cried Chanticleer, shaking his head. 'Have you never read the Bible or the Lives of the Saints? There are countless examples of dreams being sent from heaven as warnings to good Christian chickens. Don't you recall how the Pharoah of Egypt had dreams, and Joseph became prime minister because he knew what they meant. Everything the Pharoah dreamt came true. My dream had a deep and meaningful message for me – if only I knew what it was.'

Dame Pertelote spread wide her elegant and delicate toes to take a better grip of the perch. Her breast feathers were ruffled with annoyance, and her beak, as she pecked Chanticleer in the neck, was like the flashing spear of the goddess Athena. 'Prunes!' she said. 'That's what you need.'

Chanticleer spread his wings like the banners of an ancient knight riding into battle. 'O angelic hen! I had forgotten how lovely you look when you're angry – your eyes so red, your ears so fluffy, your cluck so musical! Oh queen of the coop! What is danger to a cockerel whose mate is as lovely as you? Let me take you in my wings, my pride and joy!'

Unfortunately, the perch was rather narrow for the passionate embrace, and Chanticleer tumbled off it. Picking himself up, he saw that the sun had risen and it was time to be crowing – waking the heavens with the trumpeting fanfare of his call. Chanticleer strutted out into the gardens of his palace. The nightmare beast of the firebrand tail was forgotten. What villainous monster would dare to threaten the majesty of Chanticleer? What monstrous rascal would dare to lay a paw on his regal magnificence? Chanticleer stretched his head high into the air and crowed with all his might.

There was a butterfly flitting from bank to bank of the palace grounds. Chanticleer, standing between his ornamental lake and the tall maze, vaguely composed a poem in twelve verses about the briefness of life and of butterflies in particular. The insect landed on the blossoms of a towering, scented plantation. The cockerel watched, then his sapphire feet clawed up the velvet turf of his carpeting lawn, and his black eyes shone like stars in the firmament . . .

Crouching couched in the scented plantation was the very beast of his dream – the nightmare beast of the firebrand tail – its jaws wide, its teeth

as curved and shining as the scimitars of Saladin's heathen army lying in wait for the Knights Crusader.

'Oh death, I see thy horrid shape and blazing eyes!' cried Chanticleer.

'Please don't distress yourself, sweet stately bird,' said the monster. 'I am the Knight of the Burning Firebrand, and I have travelled over furlongs and fathoms just to catch sight of the renowned, the legendary Chanticleer. I see now that the descriptions of your glory were true. Is it also true that your voice shames the thrilling trills of the nightingale? Sing, oh sing, rapturous bird and let me drink in the magical sound!'

'Ah. Well. Hm,' said Chanticleer modestly. 'By all means.' And he cleared his throat, sat back on his haunches, and stretched his neck towards the brazen disc of the rising sun.

'Cock-a-doodle-splergck-ck-ck . . .'

Glancing out of her door, the farm wife saw her cock sit up and crow on the patch of marsh grass between the duck pond and the bald privet hedge. Suddenly, out of the mint bed, jumped a bony red fox. It grabbed the cock by its neck and ran off as fast as it could go.

O listen and believe what grieving there was among the ladies of the royal court of Chanticleer. 'Our Lord has been seized by the Nightmare Beast of the Firebrand Tail!' cried Madam Pertelote. 'O paint the sun black and never let there never be another worm eaten for breakfast! O woe and double woe!'

Meanwhile, the farmer's wife grabbed up her broom and called her two girls and old Mr Talbot and Colly the dog, and they all splashed through the farmyard puddles and over the stile, shouting and hollering at the thieving fox. 'Put that bird down! Let go, you mangy animal! If you don't let that cock go this very minute, I'll knock your shaggy ears off with this broom, just see if I don't!'

You never heard such a racket. You'd have thought all the devils had got loose from hell or that a mob of vandals was burning down the town. There was never a chase to match it – across a ploughed field and uphill to the wood.

Chanticleer, banging up and down on the fox's back, had all the breath knocked out of him and was as good as dead. But at last he managed to splutter, 'You've got 'em licked, you cunning old beast, you. I've got to hand it to you: they won't catch you if they run all morning. You could turn round and stick your tongue out at them and they'd still not catch you.'

'He's not wrong,' thought the fox, and he turned in his tracks to put his tongue out at the people chasing him.

Of course, the cockerel fell out of his mouth at once, and fluttered up to the safety of a tree branch. 'Dammit,' said the fox.

O listen and lend ear to the sermon Chanticleer preached from his pulpit high in the tree. 'O ignoble and dastardly fox. Shame! Shame on you and your tribe for your violence and treason against the royal name of Chanticleer. Did you suppose that a life of crime would be rewarded with roast meat and a full stomach? No indeed! You the fox have been outfoxed. Never again will your teeth have the privilege of sinking themselves in the mantle of my feathers!'

'Ah, go on,' said the fox. 'Jump down and give us another song.'

'You're joking,' said Chanticleer. '*Semel insanivimus omnes.* That's Latin. It means, 'What kind of a dumb-cluck do you take me for?'

At the end of his tale, Brother John winked in my direction. 'You're an educated man and a poet, Master Chaucer. Did you like my little effort?'

I returned him a wry grin. 'So that's what you think of us poets, is it?'

But the Prioress leaned across, then patted her priest on the wrist. 'That was very nice, John dear. *Très gentil.*'

The Miller breathed out through his teeth, but did not have enough long words in his red head to say anything brilliantly insulting.

ALL this time, Oswald the Reeve had been skulking and sulking around on the skirts of the party, muttering and sputtering with unspent anger.

At last he thrust his horse back in among us and commented aloud to himself in a large voice, 'I suppose nobody wants to hear *my* story. The Miller's slanderous rubbish, yes, but not *my* story.'

There was a satanic gleam in his bulging eyes that told me the Reeve had more in mind than the competition in wanting to tell a story. He had been nursing the insult paid him by Matt, and now he was back for revenge.

'Feel free,' said Harry. 'Go right ahead. We're all ears.'

The Miller's horse gave a grunt as Matt rose in his stirrups to brandish himself like a torch. 'Better keep off the subject of millers, though, if you know what's good for you, Oswald!'

36

'Now it's funny you should say that,' said Oswald, 'but the story I have in mind does make passing mention of a miller. Still this fellow's a rascal. I mean, he steals from his customers – gives them short measure back after he's ground their corn for them. And everybody knows that *you* wouldn't do that – not *you*, Matt. I can't think what they mean back home when they say you dip your thumb in every sack. Everyone knows what honest fellows you millers are . . .'

We pilgrims burst out laughing, each of us thinking how inexplicably *rich* all the millers are that we know. *When did you ever see a poor miller?* – isn't that how the saying goes?

Matt gave a threatening growl, but Oswald felt safe now, circled about by an audience of pilgrims. He launched into his tale with grinning gusto.

A Racket at the Mill

THERE was once a crook of a miller called Matthew. He owned the only mill for miles around, so that he could rob his customers daily, and still they had to bring their corn to him for grinding.

But there were two students, Bright and Spark, living locally. They decided that they had brains enough between them to outwit the old scoundrel and pay him back for some of his double-dealing. (How could they know that a miller's not just as greedy as a hole in the ground, but as slippery as a handful of butter as well?)

Bright and Spark brought their corn to the mill on horseback, and set it down – two big sacks filled to bursting – by the millstone. Then they sat down on the floor.

'That's all right, boys,' said Matthew. 'No need to hang around. I'll call you when it's ready.'

'We'll stay, thank you,' they replied, and fixed their eyes on the miller as if to say, 'Now steal one grain if you can!'

If Matthew was vexed, it did not show. He set about his work, whistling tunelessly. 'Oh, look at that now,' he interrupted himself. 'I've started work without an apron.' And he slipped downstairs on the excuse of fetching one. Untying the reins of the two horses at the hitching rail, he gave their rumps such a thwack that they did not stop running until they were five fields away.

Then Matthew returned to his mill-room and observed nonchalantly to Bright and Spark, 'Surely you didn't come on foot with such a heavy load?'

'No,' they said, 'On horseback.'

'Well where did you put them? I saw no horses in the yard . . .'

It took them all afternoon to catch their animals, and by the time they crawled back to the mill, Matthew had finished grinding their corn and stood at the door, his thumbs tucked in the armholes of his smock. At his feet lay a saggy, half-empty sack. 'How tedious for you, boys. I wonder how they got loose. Still, here's your flour – and finer ground than you'd get from any mill in the South of England!'

'But we brought two big sacks of corn!' Spark protested despairingly.

'Ah, well. Lots of husks, you know. An awful lot of husks on that breed of corn.'

Bright glared murderously at the miller, but what could he say? A miller would lay his hand on the Bible and swear a cow had five legs. So Bright and Spark took their miserable scraping of flour, and left.

They did not go far. From the end of the lane, they doubled back and hid in the miller's barn till nightfall. While clouds smothered the moon, they crept into the house, and up to the miller's bedroom.

A new baby was snuffling and scratching in the crib at the foot of one bed: the bed of the miller's wife, of course. In the other, Matthew lay tangled in blankets like a pig in a parcel, snoring.

In bare feet, Spark and Bright crept to the cot and lifted it across the room to the foot of the miller's bed. Then they padded back to the door and coughed and rattled the latch and said, 'Burgle burgle burgle,' in low voices.

Matthew only turned over in his sleep and sucked his thumb. But his wife's eyes opened as wide as sunflowers, and she kicked off the blankets. She was a huge woman, and when she lifted the distaff that stood against the wall, she was as huge and white as a ship's foresail with the bowsprit in front.

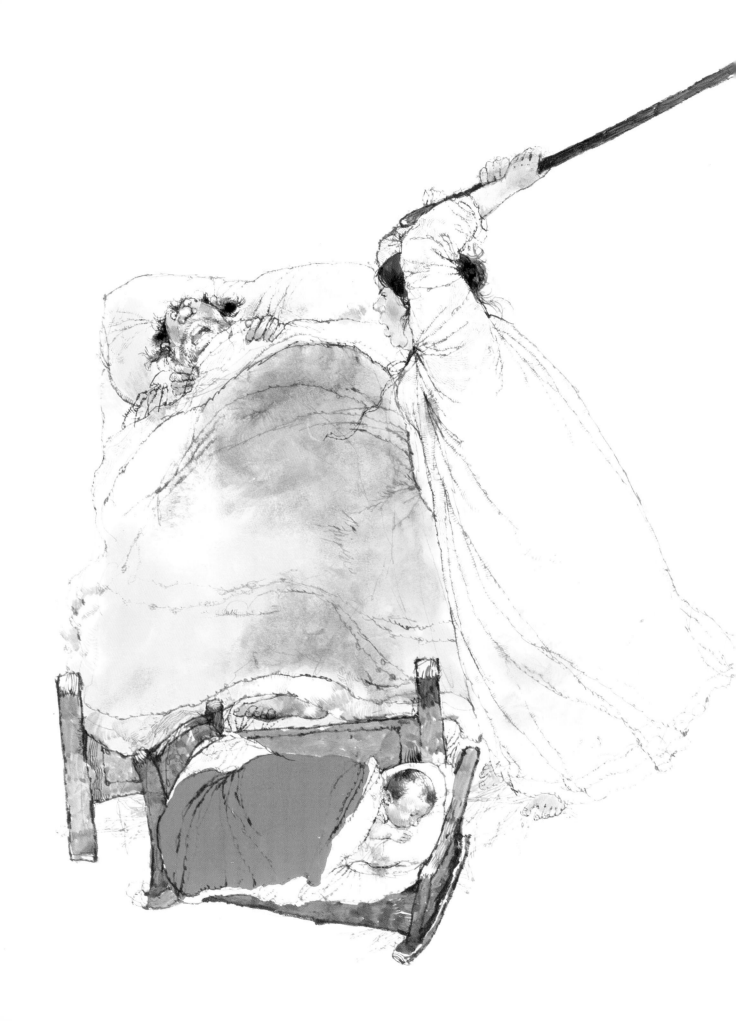

Through the house she crept, in search of the burglars. But Bright and Spark were giggling together in the press, and she found no one. Only when she returned to the bedroom did she see . . . the crib . . . at the foot of the bed . . . and a shape in the bed!

She raised such a hullabaloo that the mill-race froze in terror. 'Hide in my bed, would you, you villain? Hide in my own bed! There–take *that* for your impudence – and THAT for your villainy – and THAT for your burglary . . .'

As Bright and Spark crept down the stairs, the miller's whimpers were rising to a roar punctuated by the blows from the distaff and the wife's furious shrieks ' . . . and THAT for the shame you've brought on your poor mother . . . and *THAT* . . .'

They left hastily, but not so hastily as to leave behind two fat sacks of flour from the miller's own larder!

I hope I told that correctly. I admit, I had some trouble *hearing* the Reeve's story. This might have had something to do with the Miller playing his bagpipes all the way through it.

As Oswald finished his story, he rode, with dignity, up to Matt, and asked if he could borrow the bagpipes. 'Just for a moment, dear friend.'

Matt handed them over warily, knowing Oswald would never dare to hit him with them.

We were just then crossing the river. As Oswald trotted over the bridge, he tossed the pipes lightly over the wall. They sank with a splash, then bobbed to the surface again and sailed downstream as stately as a Viking funeral ship.

'They put me in mind,' said the Sea Captain sentimentally, 'of a privateer's schooner I once sank in the Skagerrak.'

The Parson went and retrieved them.

When the Hundred of Hoo came into sight, we had lunch at an inn. Since the incident with the bagpipes, several of us had been asking the Sea Captain for a story. We relished the idea of a sailor's yarn – of pirates and sharks and the like.

He told us a long story about a careful merchant and his wife who overspent on the housekeeping. There was not one drop of the sea in it. The Merchant said it was wonderful – a great contribution to the body of English literature. Personally, I would have preferred a pirate story.

THE troop of horses straggled out, single-file, picking their way among deep, boggy cart ruts, then forked left at a signpost. We looked round just in time to see one poor, thin beast shambling off on the other road. Its rider, the Scholar from Oxford, had his head in a book and was quite unaware of losing us.

42

Harry Bailey shook his head. 'He'd be in Maidstone before he even noticed,' he said, then galloped off to haul the Scholar's pony back into line. 'Now come on, lad. Set your studies to one side. There's a time and place for everything – and this is the time and here's the place for your story. Don't say you don't know any – the way you read, you must have seen every word a pen ever wrote!'

The Scholar looked round at us – as vague as a man just woken from a deep sleep. 'Look at that, bless him,' said the Widow-in-the-Hat. 'I don't suppose he's remembered to wash his neck or eat a bite of food since he opened that book. What's so good about it, love? You can't put it down! Is it naughty, ha-ha-ha?'

The Scholar blushed and held up the book. 'It's only *Mathematical Astronomy*.' He blinked like an owl at us until Harry reminded him about the competition. Then he said, 'Well, if you care for a contribution from someone so inarticulate and lacking in proficient handling of the dramatic forms fundamental to the narrative tradition . . .'

'Is he talking Latin?' said the Yeoman.

'No,' said Hubert, 'but I'll be damned if it's the English my mother taught me.'

The Scholar blushed again and went back to his book.

'Tell us a story, boy, and keep your long words for impressing your pupils,' said Harry clapping the Scholar on the back. His thin-shanks pony buckled at the knees. Obviously the lad spent his money on books before clothes for himself or hay for his horse.

'I went to Italy last year,' he said slowly, as if he was picking the easiest words he knew. 'And I read a story while I was there. Would you like to hear that one?'

A cheer went up from the troop of riders.

'What did he say?' asked the Widow-in-the-Hat.

The Test of a Good Wife

LORD Walter was strong, handsome and accomplished – like his father before him. When he came to power over his little province, the peasants and farmers who had served his father were proud to be owned by him. They paid their tithes and doffed their caps to him, and waited to see whether Walter would, in turn, have a son. Just as the seasons came and went, so came and went the generations of lords at the manor house.

But after a while, the people grew restless. Walter showed no sign of marrying. And without a wife, how could he have a son to follow him? The people of the estate screwed up their courage and suggested to Walter that he really ought to be getting married.

'Oh. I never thought of it,' said Walter. 'I suppose you're right!' And the people breathed a sigh of relief and looked forward to the wedding.

Preparations were made. 'A feast for two hundred!' said the cooks to tradesmen at the back door of the manor house.

'He's bought jewels fit for a princess!' the tradesmen told their wives.

'He's sent to Padua for a silk wedding gown!' said the gossiping women.

'But *who* is he going to marry?'

On the day arranged, Walter set out with a cavalcade of fifty men and women, all in their best clothes – as if he was going to meet his bride. At the edge of his estates, he halted his horse outside a patched, broken-down, rain-leaky hovel.

For it was not quite true that Walter had not thought of marrying. He

44

had once said to himself, as he rode past this old cottage on his estate, 'If ever I married, it would be to Griselda.'

Besides her beauty, Griselda had every quality perfect in the eyes of a man. She never stopped working: spinning wool, washing, tending her father's few scraggy sheep. She never giggled or gossiped like other teenage girls. She never lost her temper when things went wrong. It was as if a lifetime's wisdom and peacefulness had found its way into her head while she was still young. Best of all, she had never been heard to complain – even when she tore her only miserable dress on a thornbush; even when her overworked hands were blue with cold; even when she had not eaten for two days.

So Walter dismounted beside Griselda's house, took her old father to one side and asked his permission to marry the girl.

Poor old man, he was too astonished to speak. And before he could collect his wits, he was sitting at table in his damply draughty house, with his lord on one side and his daughter on the other.

Griselda, who did not understand what was happening, sat with her hands in her lap, her eyes on her hands, and never once looked up.

'Griselda, I've decided I'd like to marry you,' said Walter in a businesslike way. 'I've asked your father, but have you anything to say?'

'My lord!' whispered Griselda, 'I and everybody in the province already belong to you body and soul. Whatever you want, I want.'

'Good,' said Walter. 'I know it's rather unusual for someone of my standing to take someone so shabby and poor and unimportant, but I do assure you that I've thought about it. There is just one thing.'

'My lord, you do me far too great an honour . . .'

'Yes, yes. Never mind that. Promise me that my word will always be final in everything. When I say yes, you must never say no – not by so much as a frown. I hate complaining women. Agreed?'

'My lord! Who am I to cross you in anything?' whispered Griselda. 'You honour me too deeply.'

'Yes, yes. That's settled then. Ladies!'

In came the ladies-in-waiting with the silken wedding dress. And they took off Griselda's dress – holding it at arm's length and with their lips curled back in disgust – and dressed her for her wedding. With her golden hair brushed, and a crown on her head, Griselda was so transformed that the neighbours themselves hardly recognized her. 'Isn't she the luckiest woman in all Christendom?' they said to her old father as they watched the procession move off.

But he only shook his head and said: 'No good can come of such a thing,' and turned back into his doorway.

She made a radiant bride – a fairy-tale wife for the handsome lord. And when a baby daughter was born to her, she made a perfect mother, too. People came from all over Italy just to see her. When Walter was away, Griselda would take his place in settling disputes and lawsuits. She was so just and fair that they said she must have been sent from heaven to make Walter the perfect helpmate.

Then the tests began.

Walter, who had never known what it was to have a *bad* wife, began to wonder whether Griselda was really as perfect as she seemed. 'She always agrees with me,' he thought, 'but then I'm always right, so of course she would. What if I were to ask of her something really . . .'

One day, as Griselda sang their lovely daughter to sleep, a brutish-looking servant came in. 'Your husband has sent me to take away the baby,' he said, 'because of the bad-feeling among his people.'

'Bad-feeling?' said Griselda, who knew full well how much everyone loved her and her tiny daughter.

'Bad-feeling, yes ma'am, against you and the little girl – on account of you being no better than a peasant by birth.'

The young mother looked at her baby sleeping in the crib, but Griselda's face showed nothing of what she was thinking. 'Walter knows best,' she said. 'Do whatever he told you to do.'

The servant bit his lip and shuffled his boots on the floor. Then he snatched up the baby as if he would kill her then and there, but tucked her under his arm and strode out of the manor house.

Next morning, Griselda greeted Walter at breakfast with her usual smiling cheerfulness and went about her day as if her little daughter had never existed. She was never again heard to mention the little one's name.

But perhaps, when the baby boy was born to her, she had twice the reason to love and cherish him.

Walter now had what he and the people wanted most – an heir to inherit the manor and estates and the family's noble title. Delightedly he watched the boy sit up, crawl, stand, toddle and speak his first words – before the old cruelty took hold of Walter again.

'Madam,' said the serving-man, slamming into the bedroom and grabbing up the boy in his two fists. 'Your husband sent me to take away the boy because of the unhappiness he's causing.'

'Unhappiness?' gasped Griselda, who knew how dearly everyone loved the little lad.

'Your husband's bounden people are unhappy thinking that your boy might one day become lord over them – him being no better than a peasant, thanks to his mother. That's what your lord and husband says, lady.'

'Can such a small boy cause such a great unhappiness?' said Griselda, taking her son's face between her hands to calm his crying. 'Well, if my good lord thinks so, you must do as he tells you. Who am I to argue?'

After the servant had shut the door behind him, Griselda never spoke her son's name again, or shed a tear.

'What a wife!' thought Walter gloatingly. 'What a good, obedient, loyal wife! I know how much she loved those children of hers.'

And then he thought, 'Of course I've given her a life of luxury here that she would never have had with her father. I suppose she would say and do almost anything to keep her fine clothes and her soft bed. I wonder how she would behave if I . . .'

The idea stayed with him, played on him, preyed on him for week after month after year. In the end, the temptation was too strong.

He announced publicly that he was divorcing his wife.

'I'm sorry, Griselda, but the people in my villages and on my farms just can't stand the sight of you any more. They call you a "washer-woman-in-velvet", a "skivvy-in-silk". It just cannot go on.'

Griselda, her hands linked in front of her, her face a little pale, her calm eyes expressing nothing, bowed her head and said: 'No, of course, Walter. You must marry again – someone young and well-born. I am very sorry to have upset your people.'

'Well I can't have two wives, can I?' Walter blustered. 'You had better go back to your father – and give me back everything I gave you on your wedding day.'

'I can give you back my wedding ring and my jewels, lord,' said Griselda quietly, 'and leave all the fine dresses in the chests upstairs. But your ladies-in-waiting burned my old ragged dress. Leave me at least the dress I stand up in.'

Walter turned his back so as to grin and congratulate himself on choosing such a wife, such a matchless wife. There was a thrill in the pit of his stomach like the one he felt when his arrow pierced a deer he was hunting. 'How far can I go?' he wondered, and he said, 'My new wife might want to wear that dress you have on.'

So Griselda unlaced her sleeves of brocade, and velvet dress, and let them fall at her feet. 'You may keep the petticoat,' said Walter, though his throat was tight and dry. As Griselda turned to begin her long, barefoot journey home, he called her back. 'Oh, Griselda!'

'Yes, husband of mine?'

'I'll need someone to organize the wedding, and you know how to handle the servants better than anyone. You won't mind helping out, will you?'

There were angry murmurings from the peasants and farmers as Griselda walked home to her father's shambledown hut. 'They do say Lord Walter *murdered* his baby daughter,' said one milk-maid to another.

'And his little boy, too,' the other replied.

'You can see what he thinks of us working folk,' said a young farrier. 'Not good enough for his fine company. He'll marry a princess next time, you just wait and see.'

But soon they grew excited by the preparations for the wedding, and they forgot the way Walter had treated Griselda. She hid her shabby misery in her father's split and patchless hut. And because she never complained, because she smiled as much as ever, they foolishly supposed that she was happy.

'A feast for three hundred people!' said the cooks to the tradesmen at the back door of the manor house.

'Jewels fit for a queen!'

'He's sent to Padua for silk and Brittany for the finest lace.'

'And he's sent to Brescia for the bride. She's only fifteen!'

On the day of the wedding, no one was busier than Griselda. She added the final seasonings to the sauces. She sprinkled flower petals in the finger-bowls of water. She polished the marriage cup that bride and groom would drink from. Then she greeted the guests at the door – and was so charming and gracious that they wondered where a raggedy scullery maid had come by such manners.

Winding through the vineyards and meadows came the lavish procession of Walter fetching home his bride-to-be. Her young brother – a boy of about ten – rode on a dappled pony: he wore a scarlet suit, and his curled hair sprang on his shoulders. The bride herself rode in a white covered carriage hung with curtains, while her ladies-in-waiting rode side-saddle, sadly watching their hems sweep in the dust and mud.

'What do you think of my bride-to-be, Griselda?' called Walter as he rode past her in the gateway.

'She's very fair. My heart jumps strangely at the sight of her.'

'And do you wish me joy, Griselda?' he taunted.

'As much as always, my lord.'

Walter had to turn his back to conceal his pride and joy. 'Such an exceptional wife,' he thought crowingly. 'A wife in a million.' But he said, 'You give us your blessing then, do you, my one-time wife?'

'Of course, my lord. Who am I for you to seek such a blessing? But I would like to say one thing. I do not believe your new wife's upbringing was the same as mine. She's delicate and sensitive – not used to hardship and suffering. She might find your tests harder to bear than I did. I do most humbly beg you – be kinder to *this* wife.'

Only then did Walter call an end to his long joke. 'Griselda! Wife of mine! Go and dress yourself in your finest clothes and sit with me at the head of the table where a wife ought to sit. All this was just a test to see if you would keep your promise and agree with everything I said and did. This new "bride" of mine could not marry me even if I wanted her to: she's our own daughter – and this is our own fine son!'

The children stared at their mother – a stranger to them in her grey-haired middle-age. And their mother stared back at them until she fell down in a dead faint. She came round in Walter's arms.

'I sent them to Brescia,' he was saying, 'and had them educated by the best tutors in Italy. They wanted for nothing. Get up, my dear wife. I never had any intention of replacing you!'

'Did you not, my dear?'

'No! What kind of husband do you take me for? Why, a man never had a better wife!'

And the feast to celebrate the reuniting of Griselda and Walter as man and wife, mother and father, was grander than any wedding breakfast. Everyone was invited – even Griselda's old father who never went home again to his rain-leaky cottage on the borders of the estate.

'Of course it could never happen nowadays,' said the Oxford Scholar wistfully. 'Women aren't what they used to be . . .' He was just then knocked from his saddle. The Widow-in-the-Hat had given him such a hearty shove that he landed in a cart rut like a duck in a pond.

'I should just think not!' she bellowed at him as he struggled, dazed, to his feet. 'I should just think women aren't the same nowadays. They've got more sense and they've got more spirit! "Never had a better wife!" No woman ever had a worse husband, by the sounds of it, poor lamb. What am I saying, "poor lamb"? Your Griselda's a disgrace to her sex. Every woman should know how to put her husband in his place. And a husband's place is in the wrong! And what about those poor little children – grew up without a mother's love and tenderness, all on their own in some *foreign* place . . .'

Harry Bailey held up his hand. 'It was only a story, lady!' he exclaimed, trying to pacify the Widow whose hat was shaking from stem to stern with indignation. 'None of it really happened!'

'I should hope NOT!' puffed the Widow, calming down, 'I'd have no patience with a woman like that. A wife's got a duty to her husband. *I* always did my duty by all my five husbands. I nagged them when they needed to be nagged (which was eight days a week) and I licked them into shape as best a poor, weak woman could. And if any of them had lived long enough, poor souls, they would have thanked me for it!'

'I'm sure our friend the Scholar would agree with every word of that,' said Harry, trying desperately to keep the peace.

But the Scholar had opened his book again and was already engrossed in *Mathematical Astronomy*.

53

'YOU'RE clearly a woman after my own heart!' called the Monk, cantering up to the Widow's side.

'I'm after nobody's heart, you rascally womanizer! I've won the hearts of five husbands, and that's enough to weary any woman. Now I'm free to think and say what I like, thanks be to God.' She eased a heavy rug around her ample hips, and her plump legs poked forwards in the stirrups. She was wearing red woollen stockings and soft leather shoes. I suspect she was richer than all the rest of us put together.

The Pardoner suspected the same thing. He edged closer, clearly intending to sponge money from her. 'Speak up, young man!' she bawled at him. 'Or is it young lady?'

The Pardoner was hardened to insults by years of scrounging. 'I see your five husbands left you well provided for, madam. I daresay you could afford to pay for a glimpse of the treasures I've got in this bag of mine . . .'

'*Provided for?*' The Widow was incensed. 'I earned my bacon, I'll have you know, you long-haired gelding!' (The merchant told me later that she had earned her money in the weaving trade, her looms producing the best woollen cloth in Bath.) 'And as for your *treasures*,' she was telling the Pardoner, whose fawning grin was starting to droop, 'no man of mine ever kept his treasures in a bag . . . nor did I ever pay to look at them! The only treasure a woman can give a man is to love him as a cat loves her kittens – with the rough of her tongue. And the only treasure a man can bring a woman is . . . well, you all know what *that* is.'

'Oh to be sure!' said the Monk, leering. 'A kiss and a squeeze!'

The Knight's son was shocked. 'Really, sir! From a man of the church, too! Of course the lady didn't mean that!'

'Well and what did I mean, chuck?' asked the Widow kindly.

'The only treasures a man can bring a lady are his love and adoration,' said the Squire solemnly.

She looked at him fondly, reached out and tousled his curly hair. 'Bless you, son. Haven't you heard the old story? I'll tell you what a woman wants most from her man.'

What Women Most Desire

IN the old days of glory, when King Arthur's Round Table stood in Camelot, chivalrous knights sat and talked of Love. Damsels embroidered tokens of Love. Squires composed Love songs, and jousts were fought over Love. Hardly a word was spoken that was not of Love. Only when men and women *met* did they talk about the weather instead.

'How blue the sky is, lady,' a young man would say.

'And how warm the breeze,' she would reply.

'And how is your mother?' he would ask.

'Quite well, considering the weather,' she would answer.

Then he would bow, and she would smile, and they would go their separate ways.

So it was at Camelot until the hot-blooded Sir Salvio met one day with a lady in a wood.

'How blue the sky is today,' said the lady, smiling encouragingly.

'Almost as blue as your lovely eyes, lady,' he said.

The lady blushed. 'How prettily the water glistens in the brook.'

'Almost as sweet to taste as a kiss of your lips,' said the knight, and he helped himself to a kiss. The lady picked up her green skirts, and shrieked and swooped like a parrot in and out of the trees, all the way back to the Court.

So the over-romantic knight was summoned before the assembly of the Round Table. 'This most starless of knights,' said King Arthur, 'has cast his shadow over an honourable lady in the wood. What punishment should he suffer?'

In one voice, the Knights cried, 'DEATH! Cut off his head!'

Sir Salvio was most dismayed. But he bowed low from the waist, and Arthur unsheathed his sword.

'One last question,' said the knight, straightening up again. 'Perhaps the excellent Queen Guinevere can tell me: what exactly did I *do* to offend the lady in the wood?'

'What did you *do*?' exclaimed the Queen. 'You spoke of kisses when you should have been talking about the weather!'

'Ah. I see.' Sir Salvio sighed and bowed from the waist again. 'I don't think I understand women.' The shadow of the sword touched his bare neck.

The ladies of the court began to faint. Like swathes of corn behind a sickle, they fell daintily to the floor. The Queen herself looked with regret

on Sir Salvio. His hair was the colour of powdered sage and as curly as the tendrils of a honeysuckle. 'Well, well,' she said, fluttering her hands. 'Since this young man seeks to understand women, let him answer me this riddle. Let him tell me What Women Most Desire, and he shall live.'

Arthur leaned wearily on his sword. 'You have one year and a day, boy, in which to discover What Women Most Desire.'

As Sir Salvio left the Court, his knees trembled and his heart still pounded. What chance did he stand of answering the Queen's riddle? What man can guess what a woman is thinking? 'What do Women Most Desire?' he pondered, as his horse shambled along the country roads. 'Beauty, surely.'

But then he remembered money. Surely women wanted gold more than anything in the world.

He passed a young farm girl on the road, arm-in-arm with a shepherd. 'Tell me, good girl, what do you want most in this world – to be rich or to be beautiful?'

The farm girl hung more heavily on the shepherd's arm and sighed. 'Neither, sir. All I want is to be married!'

'Aha!' The knight took out a quill, and wrote on the sleeve of his shirt. Then he turned back, thinking to take the answer to the Queen at once.

On the way, he passed a convent where nuns, as white as cannikins of milk in the morning sun, were tending a field of beans. 'What that girl told me cannot be true,' thought Sir Salvio with dismay. 'So many women choose to live unmarried!'

Just then, he passed a roadside shrine. In front of it, a woman was down on her knees praying fervently.

'Forgive me interrupting your prayers,' said Sir Salvio, 'but what is it that you ask so earnestly of God?'

The woman got painfully to her feet and took up her baskets again. 'Only what every woman wants, I suppose,' she said bitterly. 'I want to have a baby.'

'Aha!' he said, and noted her words on his sleeve.

By sunset, there were twelve other notes written below it.

Sir Salvio's heart sank lower and lower. Only one answer could be right. How was he to choose it from the rest? He fingered his bare neck and thought of the sword awaiting it.

Farther and farther afield he travelled. Taking ship, he sailed to a hot and passionate country where gypsy women dressed in scarlet, and their dark skin sweated as they danced tarantellas under a tambourine moon. 'What do Women Most Desire?' he asked a girl as she whirled past his stirrup, tossing her lace-edged petticoats.

'Fun, of course!' cried the gypsy. 'Fun and laughter and love and music and passion and the clash of the moon and the spark of the stars, and to stay young for ever!'

'Thank you *very* much.' He could find no scrap of sleeve on which to write all her answers.

On and on he travelled, through lands of ice where women would not part their frozen lips to answer him – through wastelands where all the women wanted was the next meal for their children. Finally time ran short, and he turned back to keep his appointment with the King's deadline. To be one day late at Camelot would dishonour him, for the other knights would think he was fearful of the sword's edge.

So it was that he came to be riding at a gallop through the Forests of Dean on the last day, when he saw an old crone boiling up water in a cauldron.

'Old woman!' he shouted out. 'Boil my shirt, for I have slept in it this year past, and today I must present myself before the Queen of England.' He handed her the shirt on which he had scrawled the answer of every woman he had met.

The old hag held up each sleeve in turn. 'What's this, then?' she lisped through two black teeth. '*Love, Money, Passion, Power, Beauty, Children, Long life, Fame* . . . These are the stuff of women's wishes!'

'Mind your own business, weasely one, and boil the shirt. I'm sick and tired of asking What Women Most Desire.'

The shirt plunged into the cauldron, and the bubbles that rose gave strangely feminine sighs.

'What Women Most Desire? Oh, I can tell you *that*, lording. But my answer has a price. What I desire most is to marry a handsome knight with hair of just your colour and curls of just your kind. If I were to tell you the answer, you would have to marry me.'

'I'd gladly marry even you, Dame Cockroach, for the sake of the *right* answer. But I've heard so many now, that I daresay I've already heard yours from someone else.'

The old crone shrugged her humped shoulders and gave him back his shirt, dripping and steaming. 'What Women Most Desire is to have their own way in everything,' she said.

'Fine, fine.' Sir Salvio galloped off, intent on keeping his appointment with the Queen.

Knee to knee at the Round Table, the Knights of King Arthur sat playing cards. The ladies sat talking of Love among themselves. 'I hardly expected to see you again, boy,' said the King. The women's chatter subsided. The Knights at the Table turned to listen.

'And have you found an answer to my riddle?' asked the Queen.

Sir Salvio knelt and kissed the hem of her robe. 'Madam, I have a thousand.' Then he searched his shirtsleeves for just one that might save his life. But the shining whiteness of the linen almost blinded him, and just as the sleeves were clean of words, so was his memory a blank. The only answer he could recollect was the last one he had been told. '*What Women Most Desire is to have their own way in everything.*'

'Oh! Sorcery!' squeaked the Queen in delicious horror. 'No *man* ever worked that out for himself! I'm glad you have saved your life, Sir Salvio, for your hair *is* the colour of powdered sage and as curly as the tendrils of the honeysuckle. But *who told you the answer*?'

'I did, Queen Guinevere,' croaked an elderly voice. And there, perched on the back of the knight's horse where it stood tethered by the door, was the old forest crone. Her legs were as thin and knobbled as a chicken's. Here and there she had hair, but it grew only where it should not. The ladies of the Court put their handkerchiefs to their mouths and gave little cries of distaste. 'I told this fair knight the answer, and in return he promised to marry me . . . Don't look so surprised to see me, sweetheart. I jumped up behind you as you put on your shirt. I did not want to delay our marriage by so much as a single day.'

In a gesture of wild despair, Sir Salvio threw himself headlong at King Arthur's feet. 'Lord, be merciful and cut off my head here and now! For life will be worse than death if I have to marry this . . . this . . .'

'Sir!' The Queen's voice was loud and forbidding. 'Kindly remember that chivalry is the first law of this Court!'

But the knight bared his neck and thrust his sword into King Arthur's hand. '*Please* cut off my head, your majesty!'

Like a monstrous land crab, half in and half out of its skin, the hag limped forward. 'Nay, for that would deprive me of my reward. I claim my husband, and the law must give him to me!'

Then Sir Salvio threw himself at her pigeon-toed feet. 'Take my horse, take my sword – my armour. Take everything I own in the world, but spare my body! You don't know how I have dreamed of one day tasting love in the arms of a young and lovely wife!'

The antique bride gave one wild shriek of laughter and linked her arm through his. 'I am yours to command now, husband,' she said. 'Yours as much as your horse or your sword or the shirt on your back!'

Then the King joined the hands of the bride and groom. 'I give you the White Wing of Camelot for your nuptial home.'

Never was there a wedding celebrated with fewer smiles and less dancing. The groom led his bride directly to the White Wing, thinking to hide his shame within its walls. At the foot of the stairs, she tugged on his arm. 'This is the threshold of our home,' she said in a voice that crackled like burning stubble. 'So lift me in your arms and carry me over the threshold.'

Sharp with bones and as heavy as brass, she weighed like a ship's anchor in his arms, but he carried her to their bedchamber and laid her on the white bed. 'I'll sleep in the next room, lady.'

'Nay, for then we would not be married! Man and wife should sleep in the same bed.'

Sir Salvio lay down beside her in his clothes, staring at the ceiling, and tears ran down into his ears. Beside him, she smiled a toothless and frothy smile. 'Is this any way to behave on your wedding night?' she said. 'What have I done – tell me, sweetheart – nothing but save your life by answering the Queen's riddle? What's the matter with me, love?'

'What's the matter with you?' He gave a great groan. 'Nothing you could alter, lady. You're an ugly old washerwoman, that's all.'

She gave another of those cacophonous laughs. 'Oh, is it my *ugliness*, then? Why, I thought you'd be glad!'

He lifted himself on one elbow and stared at her, his eyes blinded with tears. '*Glad?*'

'Yes, glad. A pretty wife is often a worry to a man. All the time he's away fighting, or questing, or taking his horse to the blacksmith, he has it in mind to wonder, "What is she doing now? Which of my friends is

flirting with her? Has she run off yet with my squire or my serving man?"'

He nodded his head and smiled forlornly. 'In all my travels during this last year, I have not met one pretty woman I would trust.' And he closed his eyes in despair . . .

But when he opened them again, there on the bed beside him, in a gown of green velvet that put him in mind of cedar trees, lay the lady of his dreams. Her hair was the colour of powdered honeysuckle and she smelt of sage.

Only in the days of glory, when fairies were as many as the motes of dust floating in a sunbeam, could a man have found himself married to a fairy.

'Yes, it is still I, the washerwoman from the forest,' said the fairy bride. 'And now the choice is yours. Will you have me like this, or in my other form? Shall I be ugly, but love you truly, all the days of my life. Or shall I be beautiful – and a worry to you each night of your life? Shall I be waiting here for you every evening, bent and crooked but loving and loyal? Or shall I be beautiful when I hang on your arm in the gardens and in the great moot hall when there are other eyes to wink at me? Come on, decide now and never speak of it again.'

In all his travels he had never seen so lovely a lady. Sir Salvio breathed in to claim her beauty. Yes, yes, he would have her be beautiful.

Then he suddenly thought of the white sleep he would lose lying in the White Wing of Camelot while his wife was dancing the night away with other men. He thought of how the bright light of her beauty would show up all the lines and wrinkles of his own old age, and she would tire of him. And he thought of the evil of owning a lovely wife – without owning her love!

'Lady-fairy and wife of my life,' he said at last. 'Since I learned today What Women Most Desire, I know that YOU, not I, must choose. Be beautiful or be good. It shall be as you desire.'

The fairy gave one wild whoop of laughter and put her arms around his neck. Her mouth was a well of kisses. 'Because you gave this answer,' she said, 'you may have me in my fairy shape *and* keep my love and loyalty always. I will be good and faithful and I will be always waiting for you here in the White Wing of Camelot. For never in the history of human beings has a Man learned so quickly What Women Most Desire!'

So every night the White Wing of Camelot resounded to their laughter. And during the day, Sir Salvio was the envy of every other knight. For he had a wife who never talked about the weather, and who liked nothing better than a kiss in the wood from her beloved knight!

'Fairies and wizardry!' exclaimed Hubert the Monk, with a blustering contempt. 'They're all in the past – and that's just where they belong.'

'The past? The past?' bawled the Widow. 'The fairies aren't dead and gone! It's just that they emigrated when the monks and priests outnumbered them. I'll tell you this, you scandalous man, I'd trust a leprechaun sooner than a priest. A man who won't marry knows nothing about women. And a man who knows nothing about women is more ignorant than Adam in the Garden of Eden! Give me a marrying man every time!'

Their noisy arguing woke the Magistrate with a start. 'Silence in court!' he shouted. 'That woman! If I had her in my court. Scold's bridle. Duck her in the village pond. That's what.'

The Monk and the Widow took no notice. 'Tell me,' jeered the Monk, wagging his gleaming, sun-tanned head, 'when you were married to your five unfortunate husbands, did you wear your spurs in bed?'

The Widow-in-the-Hat cupped one hand to her ear and asked, 'What did the fool say?'

'Silence in court!'

WHEN the Pardoner had been sent packing by the formidable Widow, he turned his attentions to the Knight. 'Sir! I can see you're as god-fearing a man as ever set knee to a church floor. Here you are, riding to Canterbury in the hope of a blessing, and here I am with a pack full of holy objects all honeyed over with blessings for the man who touches them. Give me a crown, and I'll let you see the head-cloth of the Holy Virgin herself – and I'll throw in a glimpse of Saint Sebastian's thigh-bone preserved in alcohol.'

'Thank you, sir,' said the Knight, who was always polite, even to fools. 'But last year I stood in Jerusalem itself and saw the garden where Our Lord Jesu was laid, and where he rose to life again. I saw the field where the Blessed George's cross flamed in the sky before the Crusaders' victory over the Infidel. I don't know but that your veil and thigh-bone would be a disappointment after that.'

The Sea Captain was much less polite. 'When I was sailing a dhow on the Red Sea, I sank a ship carrying two hundred Holy Grails, a flock of sheep's bones – and each one bottled and labelled with a different saint's name – and enough splinters from the Cross to build Noah's ark all over again. As for Our Lady's head-cloth – that's all supposing She dressed like the Widow here – I've seen enough to make sails for the English fleet!'

'Are you calling my friend a liar?' roared the Summoner, pushing his pustular nose in. The Captain reeled at the smell of raw garlic, but he was unabashed. 'Yes, I'm calling him a liar and a charlatan!'

'Ah. Well. Hm. That's all right then.' And the Summoner burst into cacophonous laugh. The Doctor took a look at Saint Sebastian's thigh-bone . . . and said it was a pig's trotter.

'Ah. Well, I bought it in good faith,' bleated the Pardoner. 'And those of you who scoff at us officers of the church will all burn in Hell.'

This threat, even coming from a straggle-haired booby, silenced everyone. The Pardoner looked round in triumph and, seeing the chance to drum up a little custom, told us a story about his favourite subject – DEATH.

Death's Murderers

THE man Snatch was slumped over a table at the Tabard Inn in Southwark – (you may know the place). He had wetted his brain in beer, and it weighed heavy. The clanging of the church bell registered dully in his ears. 'Who are they burying?' he asked.

Old Harry, the landlord, who was wiping tables close by, said, 'Don't you know? I wondered why you weren't at the funeral – him being a friend of yours. It's Colley the Fence. Caught it last Wednesday and gone today. Him and his wife and his two boys.'

'Caught what?' demanded Snatch, grasping Harry's arm.

'The Black Death, of course!'

Then another customer chimed in. 'Ay, they do say the Plague came to Combleton over yonder, and Death laid hands on every man, woman and child and carried 'em off.'

'Where? Carried them off where?' demanded Snatch, fighting his way through drink-haze like a ghost through cobwebs.

'Who knows where Death carries men off to,' said a deeply hooded character sitting in the corner of the bar, 'but he sure enough comes for every man in the end. And he's taken twice his share recently, thanks to the Plague.'

Tears of indignation started into Snatch's eyes. 'I don't see what gives Death the right to go carrying off anyone!' he slurred. 'And if you ask me, it's about time some brave soul stood up to Death and put an end to his carryings-on – his carryings-off I mean. Dip! Cut! Where are you?' And he stumbled off into the sunlight to look for his two closest friends.

Dip was at home in bed, but not for long. Snatch knocked him up and called him into the street. They met with Cut coming home from a card-game and cursing his empty pockets.

Snatch threw an arm over each friend's shoulder. 'Have you heard? Old Colley the Fence is dead. Death carried off him and all his family in a couple of days. Let's take an oath, friends, not to rest until we've tracked down this "Death" fellow and stuck a knife between his ribs. Think what the mayor and parish would pay if we brought in Death's dead body. Besides – how many purses do you think he's emptied on the dark highway, eh? Death must have made himself quite a walletful by now.'

Cut fingered his sharp penknife – the one he used for cutting purses.
Dip felt his fingers itch at the promise of rich pickings. 'We're with you,
neighbour Snatch!' they cried, and off they reeled, not the sum total of
one brain between the three of them.

They looked for Death in the graveyard, but decided he must be out hunting the living instead. They looked for Death in the fields, but he had always gone before they arrived, leaving the flowers doomed to wither and the leaves, sooner or later, to fall.

Then, as the daylight failed, they saw a small figure on the road ahead. 'We've caught him up!' cried Snatch, and they fell on the man, with flailing fists.

70

'Wait a minute! This isn't Death at all!' said Cut, letting his penknife fall. 'He's just some silly old duffer. Look at him – he's older than Methuselah!'

The old man peered at them out of the dark recesses of his hood. His face was as white and bony as a skull, with purse-string lips and eyes sunk deep in red whorls of wrinkled skin. His hands were as brown as vinegar-paper, and his back hunched over like a turtle's shell. 'What do you want with me? Don't I have enough to put up with? Can't you leave a poor blighted old creature in peace?'

'You're no good to us!' Dip said in disgust. 'We wanted Death, not some wrinkled old prune on legs!'

A bitter laugh creaked out through the creature's gappy ribs. '*You* want Death! Ah, not half as much as I do! I'm the one poor beast alive that Death can't carry off. I'm condemned to live for ever and to creep about the Earth in this worn-out old body, getting older and older and older. As for Death – I've just left him under that oak tree yonder. If you hurry, you'll find him still there.'

Cut's knife was raised again. 'So! You've had dealings with him. We'll kill you anyway!'

The fossil of a man let go a sigh that seemed to break through his brittle skin. 'Aaah, I wish you could rob me of this tedious burden, Life. You should pity me, even if you have no respect for my old age. But don't bother to batter on this prison my soul calls a body: you can't free me from it.' He shuffled out from under their raised blades, muttering, 'You're the lucky ones – you might die today!'

'Get to bed with the maggots and mould, you old relic of the Devil,' Snatch cursed. 'We're on our way to kill Death. Then no one will have to die any more!' As soon as the old man was out of sight, the three accomplices forgot him completely.

Under the oak tree, there was no sign of Death. But there was a pot of money as big as any crock of gold at the rainbow's end.

Cut tipped the jar over with his foot, and the wealth of seven life-times spilled out on to the grass. They looked around. No one was even in sight. And there had been no attempt to hide the gold. It lay there, just inviting them to keep it. Snatch and Dip and Cut were suddenly rich!

'Rich! We're rich, rich, rich!' As the gold coins spilled out of the jar, so all thought of their plot to kill Death dropped out of their minds.

'Dip, your legs are youngest,' said Snatch. 'Run into town and fetch us some wine. We've got to celebrate luck like this!'

'Why is it always me?' Dip threw a sulky look at the gold but was given only one coin to buy the makings of a party.

'We'll both stay and guard it, don't you worry,' Snatch assured him. 'Be quick, lad. When you get back we'll decide what we're to do with it all – what mansions we'll build, who to bribe, what monks we'll pay to have done in. We don't have to do our own dirty work from now on, boy! We'll be the Three Kings of the Footpads.'

Full of such thoughts, Dip set off into the dusk to buy cakes and wine. The sun was behind him, and his shadow stretched long and spidery ahead, so that he was all the time stepping into his own darkness.

Snatch and Cut watched him go, then sat down on either side of the pot of gold. They counted the coins. Somehow it always came to a different number: 848 or 916 or 772. Snatch scowled. 'Of course you realize we can't divide it three ways.'

'We can't?'

'You take my word for it. It won't share out evenly.'

'It won't?'

'Two ways, yes. Not three. One of us will have to take less.'

'Oh!'

Cut decided at once that since Dip was the youngest, he should take the smallest share. They both nodded to themselves and settled back to counting the gold. This time there seemed to be 999 – or 783, or perhaps 870. But it did not change their opinion that Dip should have less.

'Of course it won't go far between the *three* of us,' Snatch mused. 'Not with the cost of living how it is. And you know how Dip squanders money.'

'No?'

'He'll soon have spent all his, and he'll be asking to borrow from us.'

'But I can't spare any of mine!' said Cut anxiously.

'No more can I. There's little enough to share out between two, let alone three.' They lapsed into silence, and above them the oak's heavy branches groaned while the gold coins clinked between their fingers. 'Supposing . . .' said Cut, 'just supposing Dip was to meet with an accident on his way back from town . . .'

'So many footpads these days . . .' said Snatch nodding sadly. 'So many ruffians and murderers.'

Meanwhile, Dip was watching his shadow move ahead of him on the roadway like a black plough. How big it was – much bigger than him. When he had his share of the money, he would be a bigger man in every way. No more creeping through the crowds at fairs, cutting purses and catching the pennies that dropped. He could walk tall and stately, in fur-trimmed robes, and people would touch their forelocks and step

aside. Beggars
would fight for
the chance to plead with him.
And if he felt like it, he could drive
them away with a pelting of money,
and see them grovel in his wake.
Ah, but if he was going to start
giving money away, there would be less
for the true necessities – drink and women and
gambling. In fact he could think of so many good
uses for the gold that it seemed a pity Cut and
Snatch had been with him when he had found the jar.
Really, the more he thought about it, the less fair it
seemed that they had bunked in on his good fortune.
As he reached the outskirts of the town, he noticed
an apothecary's sign hanging over a door. He did not
remember ever having seen it before, but he knocked
without hesitation.
'What's your trouble, young man, that you rouse me
from my bed?' An ancient, hairless head poked out of an
upstairs window, grotesque and vaguely familiar with its
parchment-yellow shine.
'Rats,' said Dip, his head muffled up in his cloak. 'The
rats are eating me out of house and home.'
'Here. One drop of this will finish them off. Have it
for free.' The ancient apothecary must have had the
poison in his pocket, for he dropped it down at once, into
Dip's outstretched hands. 'It couldn't be simpler,' he called
as the boy hurried off to the inn.
Dip bought three bottles of wine. Every last drop of the
poison went into two of the bottles. The third he marked
carefully to be sure of telling it apart. Then he was off to
collect his rightful share
of the golden hoard –
every last coin of it.

In the pitch dark of late evening, he stumbled over Cut and Snatch snoozing under the oak tree in the deep grass. 'Thought you'd forgotten us,' said Snatch with a sort of grin.

'I wouldn't forget my two old friends, now would I?' Dip opened his bottle of wine and took a swig. 'Have a drink, why don't you?' Cut and Snatch knelt up and groped for the wine, their hands brushing Dip's face in the dark. They moved to either side of their good friend . . .

Along the road came the sudden noise of the plague cart rattling out of the town towards the lime pits in Ring-a-Rosey Hollow. They all three watched its creaking progress beneath the light of the coachmen's torches. Its white cargo of dead bodies joggled against one another like restless sleepers. A limp arm dangling through the cart rails swung to and fro, for all the world as if it was beckoning them . . .

'We took an oath to kill old Death,' said Cut, remembering.

'We'll get round to it some time,' said Snatch, drawing his dagger. 'One thing at a time.'

He plunged the knife into the back of Dip's neck. It met with the seam of his hood, and the lad looked round in astonishment in time to make out the shape of Cut, outlined against the moon. Then Cut's sharp penknife caught him under the ribs and he sprawled, cursing, to his death, among the gnarled roots of the oak tree.

'It's done,' Snatch panted, and his throat felt suddenly dry. 'Let's drink to our partnership, Cut. Where did he put the bottles?'

By feeling along the ground, they found the three bottles in the long grass. The opened one had emptied itself into the ground, but the others were intact. A bottle a-piece, Cut and Snatch sat with their backs to the oak tree, and drank to their new-found fortune.

In the morning, Death came back for his pot of gold. He wrapped it in the miserable rags of his decaying cloak, close to his gappy ribs. The three corpses under the tree made no move to stop him, and he left them to a wealth of flies and crows before continuing his endless journey. The gold weighed light in his arms. Though his bones were dry and his muscles were like the withered tendrils of a grapeless vine, his strength was immense. He could carry off the biggest or strongest of men – even though, like any man or beast, he could never carry off himself.

'Remember!' said the Pardoner, intoning through his nose in his best Sunday bleat. 'Death is only the crossroads at which we take the road UP to Heaven or DOWN to Hell!' He accompanied this with sawing movements of his hands. With his sticky white palms, and surrounded by his bottled and bagged relics, he put me in mind of a conjuror performing tricks.

But by the time the Pardoner had finished his macabre story, large numbers of pilgrims had dropped back to ride in a bunch at the rear. Comforting drink was circulating, and the cook was already flat on his back with his head lolling on the roots of his horse's tail. 'God's good mercy on us miserable sinners!' he cheered and, as the Haberdasher tried to pour wine into his mouth, choked and fell off.

'By Saint Loy, what a *nasty* story,' said Prioress Eglantine. 'My little Wuff didn't like that one *bit*.' Her lap dog accordingly growled at the Pardoner from the pommel of the nun's saddle.

But the Summoner took great delight in his friend's story, and burst into song:

> 'Sleep little, my lovely,
> And wake with a smile;
> Death is for ever,
> Life's only a while!'

The Pardoner joined in, his blond lashes straining like exclamation marks round his bulging blue eyes:

> 'Death is for ever;
> Life's only a while!'

Angrily, the Miller drowned them out with a frenzied lament on the bagpipes, and the Sea Captain could be seen on the skyline, keeping his distance until the subject of Death had been well and truly dropped.

I noticed, during the course of the afternoon, that certain of the pilgrims slipped furtive coins into the Pardoner's hand and were allowed to peep into his baggage, or touch one of his worthless fakes. I suppose that's how he carries on in the little country churches each Sunday – scaring the congregation witless with talk of Death and Hell, then letting them buy back their peace of mind with their hard-earned pennies.

Myself, I wish you *could* get nearer to Heaven by touching a bottleful of pickled pig's trotter or half an old pillowcase.

THE Pardoner and the Summoner, their arms round each other's shoulders, rolled along like two pirate ships lashed together in pitched battle. They roared songs into each other's ears like volleys of cannon fire, singing whatever the Miller played on his bagpipes, the Summoner pausing only to cram garlic cloves into his mouth and champ on them.

The Magistrate, perched forward like a parrot on a perch, trotted up to Harry with a fiercely efficient look on his face. 'Dinner? Bed?' he snapped. 'Any ideas? Horses. Getting tired.'

'I was thinking to stay the night at the Saracen's Head,' said Harry affably. 'We'll be there in half an hour.'

The Magistrate altered the length of his stirrups, then busily altered them back again. 'Must be properly organized. Some very sloppy fellows here. That cook? I'd throw him in gaol.'

'It's all in hand,' said Harry. 'Before we get there, Geoffrey here can tell us a story.'

'Right. Good. It's in hand, then? Would organize it myself. Lot to do. Lot on my mind. Yes? All right then.' And he bustled away to do something very important – or at least to think about doing it.

'I expect something good from you, Geoffrey,' said my old friend. The Ship's Captain, tossed painfully about in the saddle, asked what work I did to make me good at storytelling.

'I'm a customs officer, really,' I said. 'And a poet – in a small way.'

'By Saint Elmo!' exclaimed the Captain. 'A scribbling customs officer! I've fought pirates, and thrown them to the sharks afterwards. But the only sharks that ever robbed *me* were your accursed revenue men! Well I'll scuttle you now we're on dry land, my boyo! You could tell the thousand and one tales of the Arabian Nights and you wouldn't get *my* vote!'

I knew now that I had to think of something a little special to entertain my fellow travellers. 'I won't give you a story at all!' I exclaimed. 'I'll give you an epic poem in a hundred and seven verses. A little thing I composed last week . . .'

A Gem of a poem called 'Sir Topas'

'Hm, ahem-hm . . .

Now hark and listen to my song –
The best you ever heard –
About a knight who righted wrongs
And who to glory spurred
His brave and fiery-footed steed;
This hero of great valour
Did braver and more gallant deeds
Than any in Valhalla.

This hero's name Sir Topas was,
And in his armour bright
He quite outshone the sun because
He also shone at night.
His hair was gold as harvest wheat,
His eye as blue as sky.
His legs, which ended in his feet,
Were shapely at the thigh.

His trusty sword was polishèd
Brighter than moonshine's beam,
And from his curly-hairy head
Reared up a helmet green.
Not only was he very nice
To look at quite close-to,
You never had to ask him twice
For deeds of derring-do.

One night he lay upon his bed –
His eyes were wide and starry –
A dream had trickled through his head
Of such a lovely Fairy.
'I loved her in a twinkling, ooo!'
He sighed into his mattress,
And rising, stretching, blinking, too,
He stared out of the lattice.

'Tomorrow I shall find my love,'
He said unto the owls,
'Below the earth or up above,
In fair land or in foul!'
He left at once upon his quest,
His sword and shield in hand,
And all day long he did his best
To seek out Fairyland.

Of course he did, eventually,
But clawing through the door
Came the most elementally
Grotesque, enormous paw!
A giant guarded Fairyland
And would not let him in.
'I'm very sorry,' Topas said,
'I'll have to do you in.'

Oh, listen close and listen well!
Oh, hear how Topas fought
That oh-so-horrid giant fell-
ow called Olifaunt . . .'

'Stop! Silence! Not another word!' Harry Bailey was leaning on the pommel of his saddle, with the look of a sea-sick fisherman rearing up over the side of a rowing boat. His face was quite ashen.

'Yes, I'm sorry about that last line,' I said, 'but it was either that or change the name of the giant and I don't like to change the facts of a story *too* much . . .'

'My dear boy,' he bellowed. 'If you had any feelings of pity at all in that merciless heart of yours, you would have stopped after the first verse. Spare us your appalling doggerel! I won't have another line of that intolerable nonsense inflicted on these poor, defenceless people.'

'You mean you don't like it?' I said, rather hurt.

'Well put it this way,' said Harry, 'If you persist in the story of Sir Topas, I shall feel obliged to take off your horse's saddle-cloth and to stuff it down your throat!'

Just then, the Widow from Bath rode past me and inquired when I was going to begin. Harry told her that I had changed my mind and was not going to tell a story after all, being too ignorant to know any.

I did not argue with him.

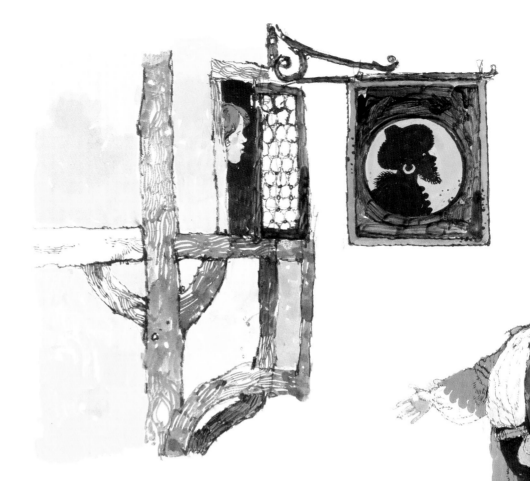

WHEN we reached the Saracen's Head, we found the doors shut and the whole house apparently abandoned. Harry rattled the latch, and the Summoner brayed out, 'Let us in! I could eat the leg off a sheep and the wool still on it!'

The Franklin seemed shocked to find the inn shut. 'My master's doors are never shut to travellers. It's my job to make sure his larder is always full, and his guests want for nothing. I keep a cold roast always on the kitchen table – in case people call in. I tell you, it *snows* food and drink when anyone visits me or my master.'

I could well believe the Franklin. He was that comfortable shape of man who enjoys good food, and his nose was cherry red from drinking. But he was not *gross* like the man who keeps the biggest helping to himself and leaves the larder bare for his friends. I envied the lord or gentleman whose household he ran.

'Open up!' yelled the Summoner, 'or I'll eat the straw in your stables and the horses after!'

'Not good enough. Really. Lack of organization,' muttered the Magistrate. 'If a thing wants doing. Better do it yourself.'

80

'It's awfully thirst-making, all this riding,' said the Cook. His saddle had slipped round, so that he was clinging to the side of his horse. There were wine stains in his hair. 'If I could just get down, I could roast a spit and build something . . . that's not right. I could build a roast and spit something . . . I could spit a build and . . .' His horse shook itself, and he slithered in a heap to the ground and made no further attempt to move.

The Summoner was bawling: 'OPEN THE DOOR OR I'LL EXCOMMUNI-CATE YOU, YOU HEATHEN SON OF A BENIGHTED INNKEEPER!'

81

The Miller was squaring up to the door with the clear intention of battering it down with his head.

An upper shutter banged open, and a pretty girl poked out her head. 'Pa's gone to Canterbury to pray for Auntie Marie who's been taken poorly.'

The Squire gripped my arm and gave a stifled exclamation. 'Did you ever see such eyes, Mister Chaucer!'

'Are you closed for business, then?' called Harry.

'Pa said not to open to the likes of him,' said the innkeeper's daughter, pointing at the Miller. 'But seeing as how there are men of the church among you, I'll come down and open.'

'Such a sweet voice!' gasped the Squire, trembling visibly.

With a shooting of bolts, the girl appeared in the doorway, laces dangling from her over-bodice. We stumbled, bow-legged, into the inn, and eased ourselves down on to the benches. The girl busied herself fetching cheeses and ham, beer and loaves, fresh cream and apples, and she set two dozen eggs to boil. When the Cook offered to help, she propped him in the corner, out of her way.

'Hospitality indeed!' the Squire told her admiringly.

'You're welcome sir.'

'It's a tasty enough *snack*,' admitted the Franklin to me, 'but I wish I had you all at my master's house now. I'd do you proud. There's no greater honour in this world than to sit with friends round your table while they eat your food.'

Next to the Franklin, the Steward was crouched over his meal, his arms circling the trencher and his mole-like hands shovelling food into his mouth. Nothing was going to go missing from *his* plate: so said the look in his shifty eyes.

'All right everyone? Satisfied?' barked the Magistrate standing up to inspect the room. He granted the meal his approval, dismissed the innkeeper's daughter, and sat down, somehow taking credit for the whole thing himself.

Then the Franklin told us his tale while we ate. He laid it before us like one of his renowned banquets, and we savoured it all the more for being sat down at table.

Love on the Rocks

ON a cliff in Brittany, on a day so calm that the sea mirrored the jagged shoreline rocks, Arviragus and Dorigen fell in love. Though Dorigen was a lady of high birth, and Arviragus was nothing but a poor knight, she promised to be his bride, and they travelled together to his home country of Penmarch.

Now who should be at the wedding but a young squire called Aurelius. When he saw Arviragus' bride, his heart was pierced deeper than a deer by an arrow. All day long, he wrote ballads and love songs. He even sang them at Arviragus' wedding party. More than one maiden swooned at the sound. More than one young girl sighed after Aurelius. For he really was a very fine shape in tunic and hose. But he had eyes only for Dorigen.

For a year or more, the newly-weds were happy. Unfortunately, Arviragus was a proud and impoverished knight. It rankled sorely with him that Dorigen's money paid for their food, their clothes, the servants wages. 'I'll go across the Channel to England,' he said, 'and come back to you a rich man.'

Dorigen pleaded with him to stay. 'What if your ship were to sink on the stormy seas? How would I know? What could I do? Don't leave me all alone and waiting!'

But nothing would dissuade him. From Brittany to Britain he sailed, and high in the castle of Penmarch, Dorigen sat thinking of him.

'You'll do yourself no good sitting at home,' said her friends. 'Come out for a walk, at least, and breathe the good sea air.'

It was a bright day, but windy. The sea broke white over the black rocks of the shore. Dorigen put her hands to her head and wailed, 'Oh, the rocks are like teeth in the mouth of a mad dog! See how they foam, and tear the sea! Look how they gnash at the ships! Supposing Arviragus is out there now! Those rocks would chew his hull and crush it, and devour all the sailors – and the passengers too! Oh take me home! I should never have come!' And her friends took her home and were three months more in comforting her.

'Your husband's safe on dry land in England,' they said. 'Come out for a picnic and remind your face how to smile!' So Dorigen agreed to go on the Mayday picnic.

Aurelius went too.

In a woodland bower splashed clean by showers, its scents spiked by Blossom sprinkled the picnickers while they ate and played chess or backgammon. After the meal, there was dancing. But Dorigen sat out every dance, wishing Arviragus was there to be her partner.

When Aurelius saw her wander off among the trees, he found an excuse to leave the dance, and followed her. She walked as far as the clifftop before noticing him. 'Aurelius, why aren't you dancing?'

'Because my heart is here, lady!' Aurelius fell to his knees and buried his face in the folds of her dress. 'Tell me, dearest, fairest Dorigen, is there no hope, no hope at all?'

'Dear me, Aurelius, whatever are you talking about?' She tried to pull her skirts away, but he only clung, with both arms, round her knees.

'Didn't you know?' he wailed.

'Know?'

'Have you never suspected?'

'*What*, Aurelius?'

'That I love you, lady.'

'But that's *absurd*.'

'Is there no hope for me?'

'Well, of course there isn't, you silly boy. I'm married. I promised to love Arviragus for ever and ever. Now do get up.'

'No! I'll throw myself off the cliff! I'll drink poison! I'll die of grief!' In
his tantrum, Aurelius rolled on to his back, like a turtle on its shell, quite

incapable of righting himself. Dorigen was embarrassed, a little flattered, and rather tempted to giggle.

'Send me through fire to fetch you cool water!' Aurelius was howling. 'Send me to the frozen north to fetch a polar bear! Send me to peel a rainbow off the sky! Send me . . .'

'Yes, yes. That's quite enough of that. I don't want to send you anywhere – except away. You're being very tiresome.' She walked to the cliff's edge and looked down. As far as the eye could see, black rocks broke through the waves and tore the surf to shreds of white. The same old fears swept back into her breast. 'I'll tell you what, Aurelius. If you could remove all the black rocks from the shores of Brittany, I'd love you all my life long, I swear it.'

'Oh,' said Aurelius flatly as he sat up. 'Is that your final word?'

'It is. Now go back and dance with the young ladies. They're all pining for you, poor dears.'

Aurelius brushed the grass off his stockings. 'I shall go home and die of a broken heart, lady.' And he picked his way through the trees with the slow dignity of a flamingo. Dorigen cast one more anxious look at the deadly black rocks where so many ships had foundered, then went back to the picnic. Aurelius had gone.

'Where have you been!' her friends greeted her. 'Wonderful news! Your husband's ship has been sighted off the coast! He'll be in harbour by nightfall!

Then Dorigen joined in the dancing. You would have thought it was her wedding day, to see how she danced.

Meanwhile, Aurelius left Penmarch with his brother to ride to Orleans . . . and to consult a magician!

They had barely reached Orleans when they passed a young stranger on the road. He called out: 'Aurelius! I know why you've come here. I can help you win the woman!' And it was true. There, on the lawns of Orleans, Aurelius and his brother sat down while the magician conjured pictures out of the hazy air.

He conjured music, too, and a vivid image of Dorigen danced alone among them, on the grass. Aurelius threw himself at the magician's feet. 'If you can do that, surely you can make the black rocks of Brittany disappear!'

'Of course. For one thousand pounds, I will cover every rock for the space of ten days, so that people will believe them gone.'

'That's long enough. It will give me time to hold Dorigen to her promise.'

'Aurelius!' cried his brother. 'One thousand pounds! Think!' But Aurelius' mind was made up. He struck the bargain.

Magic was in the moon that night as it rose over Brittany. Magic was in the throbbing light, as it dragged the water to and fro in the sink of the sea. Magic was in the high clouds and the pulsing of the stars. Out on the sea, a sailor bound for Brest leaned over the prow and stared. A shoreline he had never seen before loomed up in the moonlight . . .

Dorigen rose early, to offer up thanks in the temple for Arviragus' return. But as she knelt down, Aurelius stalked in behind her. Nervously he approached. Then his words sprang out like ambushers. 'Well? I've done it! Now you must keep your promise!'

'Done what? Aurelius, are you ill? Your eyes are so bright they frighten me!'

The young squire caught her up in his arms. 'I love you, lady. I told you as much, though you took no pity on me. Now I've removed every rock from Brittany's shore, and you must return my love for ever and ever, as you swore to do!'

Dorigen gave a shriek and, tearing herself from his grasp, ran to the clifftop. Already a noisy crowd stood shoulder to shoulder along the grassy brink, peering down with 'oos' and 'aahs'. She pushed her way through to the front and stared down in horror at the clean, gleaming rim of water that lapped high against the cliff.

'How? Oh *how*? It's unnatural! Why would the gods do this to me? What witchcraft did Aurelius use?' For a moment she stood poised on the brink, thinking to throw herself down into the grey-green sea. If she lived, she must surely keep her word to Aurelius or be shamed for ever. And if she kept her word, then too she would be shamed for ever.

There was only one thing to do. She would tell Arviragus and let him decide.

By this time, her husband had heard the amazing news: that the sea had swallowed up every black rock on Brittany's coast, and he too went up to the cliff to see for himself. Half-way there, he met his wife, her face soaked with tears. She poured out the whole story – of the picnic, of Aurelius' vows of love, of her joke about the rocks. When she had finished, she waited, her head hanging down, to hear what he would say.

Arviragus put a comforting arm round her shoulder and said, 'It won't be so terrible, my dear. Aurelius is very handsome, after all. I'm sure in time you'll come to care for him. And I shall try to be happy, knowing that you are well loved.'

'You mean I must *go* to him?'

Arviragus bit his lip. 'For the time being, we must *pretend* to go on

being married. But every night you can go by carriage to his house, and in the morning the carriage will bring you back. Only we three will know the truth – that you are his lady now and not mine. I think you should go now and put his mind at rest. After all, a promise is a promise.' He kissed her hand, and turned back towards the castle. His heart inside him was almost too heavy to carry.

Dorigen ran her fingers through her hair. She drank in the sea air as though it were a welcome cup of poison. Then she walked, with dignity, towards Aurelius' house.

Its windows were being boarded up. Its furniture and contents were being auctioned in the garden. Through crowds of dealers, agents and curious onlookers, Dorigen pressed on towards the house. She did not stop to wonder why Aurelius was selling everything he owned.

'Dorigen! What are you doing here?' Aurelius stepped out of the shadow of the wall and took her arm.

'I have come to keep the promise I made on Mayday last.'

Aurelius caught his breath. He had expected pleas and arguments. But here was Dorigen, keeping her word without a murmur of complaint. He loved her all the more for it, but his love was more gentle than before.

'I discussed the matter with my husband,' she said, 'and he agreed that there is no other way. A promise is a promise.'

'You TOLD Arviragus?'

'Of course.'

'And he agreed?'

'Of course. A promise is a promise, and he is an honourable knight.'

They stood and stared at each other, Dorigen flushed with crying, Aurelius flushed with embarrassment. He loved her all the more for her honour, but his love was more humble than before.

'You put me to shame, both of you,' he said at last. 'I cannot come between such a noble husband and wife. Please tell Arviragus that I would rather die of love than see love die between you. I release you from your promise.'

So Dorigen ran all the way home and flung herself, like a sheaf of flowers, into her husband's outstretched arms. Their happiness was unmatched and unending, and nothing nor no one ever came between them again.

As for Aurelius, he turned his attention to raising one thousand pounds. Everything would have to be sold to muster it. But never for one moment did he think of withholding the money from the magician of Orleans. After all, a bargain is a bargain. But one thing was troubling him. He took all the gold he had, and rode to Orleans.

'Here is half your fee,' he said apologetically to the young magician. 'Please, I beg you, give me some time to pay the rest. If I sell the house and all the land, there will be nowhere left for my brother to live. As for me, I don't care if I have to beg in the streets. But my brother doesn't deserve to suffer because of my foolishness.'

The conjuror peered at him. 'And have you won the lady Dorigen, thanks to my magic?'

'No, no, no. Never mind that.'

But the magician was puzzled, and wrung the whole story from Aurelius. 'It was a trick, after all,' said the squire finally. 'I didn't deserve to win her by a trick.'

Then the magician flung back his head and roared with laughter. 'My dear friend! I can't profit at the expense of a gentleman like you! I won't take a penny, no *not one penny*! It's reward enough to know there are three such noble people left in the world! Get along home – before the auctioneers sell all your best horses, and your favourite armchair, too!'

'Tell me, friends,' said the Franklin. 'Who behaved best – the squire, the magician, Dorigen, or her husband?'

'The lady, of course,' said the Ploughman in his flat, bluff country accent. 'She delivered herself into the hands of a rogue, and she didn't try to hide it from her husband. 'That's *two* good things.'

'Nonsense,' said the Widow-in-the-Hat with a jab of her elbow. As Arnie Garvus said in the story – that Horelius was a handsome young thing with a fine pair of legs. Where's the bad luck in being loved by two good-looking men?'

'Ah now, lady,' said the Knight reprovingly. 'You know you don't mean that. And you the faithfullest of wives to five husbands.'

A distant look came into the Widow's eyes, and she smiled. 'You're right, yes. I was a good, faithful wife after I married. But *before* . . . when I was a girl . . . ah, then I broke a few hearts, I can tell you. I've only got to look at that young son of yours, Sir Knight, to remember how sweet *those* days were. Hey-ho.'

We all turned to look towards the beer kegs where the Squire crouched over his flute, swaying in time to an empassioned melody. Like a snake conjured from a basket by some Moorish snake-charmer, the innkeeper's pretty daughter crept closer and closer. Their gazes were tied in a love-knot.

The Knight shook his head and sighed. '*Another* fiancée. He'll be up all night now, writing love-songs. I shan't get a wink of sleep. And by Friday week, he won't even remember the lassie's name!'

'I hope the lassie knows that,' said Harry, who had a daughter of his own and would not like her heart broken by such a fickle lover.

But as if she read his thoughts, the innkeeper's daughter glanced across the crowded ale-room and winked one bright blue eye. She had met plenty of pretty squires before, passing by on the road to Canterbury.

W E were marshalled next morning by the Magistrate who gave such a bark that the Yeoman jumped to his feet, with his big sword half drawn, and knocked his head on the roof timbers. Our upper room was still dark.

'Beetle!' cried the Magistrate when he had won everyone's attention with his tut-tutting. 'Beetle. Fell out of the thatch. Right in the mouth! Disgusting! Not another minute! Not in this place!'

We all groaned, knowing we would get no more sleep now that the Magistrate wanted to be on the road. There followed a duststorm and a plague of nits, as everyone shook out their blanket and piled it in a corner for the innkeeper's daughter to fold and put away.

As it turned out, the Magistrate, in swallowing the unfortunate beetle, got a bigger breakfast than most of us. The ladies had already risen. Downstairs the Prioress Eglantine sat at table, a napkin tucked into her wimple at the chin and her sleeves rolled right back to her white elbows. She had eaten all of any breakfast the girl had laid out for us.

Outside it was raining again. We were so disconsolate that even the apple blossoms of Ashford looked like tearful, pink-faced angels lamenting over us sorry bunch of sinners.

Then I thought of just the thing to spite that pompous little Magistrate. 'Won't you tell a story, your worship?' I said fawningly, knowing how he hated having actually to *do* anything himself.

'Oh! Well! I don't know! Lot on my mind, you know. Too busy to read much . . .' His protests were drowned by derisive calls of 'Silence in Court! Silence for the judge!'

So here is the story the Magistrate told. Don't blink or you'll miss it.

Snowy Crow

YOU know Crow – blacker than a sack's inside. He was not always so. Once he was white. No morning milk was whiter. And his song flowed like honey. He sang in a golden cage in the court of Alexander and his Queen. High in the rafters he sang. Returning home, the King would call, 'Hello, Crow. How went the day?'

'Rest assured, lord. All's well.'

From his high perch, Crow saw everything. He saw the King ride off to hunt. He saw the Queen – more beautiful than any – sit at her sewing. He saw the tradesmen come and go.

So it was that he saw the Queen's lover call for a kiss and stay for an embrace, and he heard them speak of Love! Crow's feathers then grew colder than snow, and he huddled on the floor of his cage.

'Hello, Crow. How went the day?'

But no answer came to Alexander's greeting.

'How now, Crow? What's amiss?'

'Nothing – so long as I say nothing.' Crow's voice was cracked with crying.

'Go to, Crow. I *will* know.'

'Then know that the Queen loves another far more than you.' And Crow's voice broke entirely and was never mended.

The King's heart filled like a cauldron with scalding anger. He drew his sword, and killed his Queen, and wiped the blade on her hair.

But even when she was dead, she was more beautiful than any living. For twelve long hours he stood beside her and pondered the words of the bird. Then he lowered the golden cage and tipped Crow out-of-doors. 'Oh woe, Crow! You have made me kill a lady more beautiful than any in the world. What made you lie?'

'I? Lie?'

'Aye. Lie! So, Crow, for ever more be blacker than the night to which you have brought me!'

And as he spoke, the croaking Crow shrank back – ink-black – from the King's furious gaze . . . and remained so ever after.

Quite right, too, I say. For what *good* does it do to speak the truth? People will believe what they like.

'Is that what you tell the witnesses in your courts?' asked Harry.

'Them?' snapped the Magistrate. 'They know it already. Liars every man jack of them. Pah!'

W E weren't five miles past Boughton under Blee when a solitary horse-rider came thundering towards us out of a wood. I thought he was an African at first, but his face was just plain grimy. Lagging behind him was a tattered, elderly, clerical gentleman on a rickety horse, keeping up as best he could. Both kept looking over their shoulders, and we thought nervously of footpads.

But when the leading rider saw us, he slowed his horse to a sedate trot and hailed us most politely. 'May I ride with you, masters?'

'Are you running away, young man?' asked Harry.

'Running away, sir? Me, sir? No, sir. Certainly not, sir.'

We nodded our welcomes and he pressed in among us like a playing card shuffling itself into the pack. 'You must be prepared to tell a story if you travel with us,' said Harry. 'Will the elderly gentleman be joining us, too?'

The Canon could have caught up by now, but he hung off at a distance, riding parallel to the caravan of pilgrims. He kept beckoning his servant and making 'psst' noises through his teeth. But the boy with the dirty face took no notice at all.

'Don't take this amiss,' said the Steward, 'but you seem in a mighty hurry to leave Boughton.'

'A little misunderstanding,' said the sooty servant with a foolish grin and a wave of his hand. 'A little matter of some funds which the good people invested in my master's work.'

'And what work was that?'

95

'Psst. Boy!' hissed the Canon from thirty yards away.

'My master,' said the servant quite loudly, 'is a student of that venerable and respected science of alchemy. A research scientist, you understand. The trouble is with people in these country towns, they give an alchemist money because they think he can turn their spoons to gold. But research costs money before you can expect results . . . There are materials to be paid for. Accidents happen . . .'

'Pssst!' hissed the Canon. 'Keep quiet, Peter! Come away!'

'We were very close to finding the secret. But research costs money. You're reasonable people . . . you understand that!'

'Shut up!' the Canon suddenly shrieked, standing up in his stirrups. 'Come away, Peter! Your mouth's so big you'll fall down it one day and drown!' We looked back and to, from the raggedy Canon to his servant who obstinately pretended not to hear. 'Well God quit you, boy! I'm off, before you get us both hung!' And the Canon threw one more desperate look over his shoulder, and rode off to the South, cursing his servant loudly.

The servant Peter breathed a huge sigh of relief. 'There now, masters, I'm free of him. Seven years I've worked for that old charlatan, but thanks be to God I'm free. Look at me – black in the face blowing up his infernal coals . . .'

'So you took money from people who thought you could turn lead into gold?' said the Merchant, insisting on the precise truth. 'They must have been fairly stupid to think your master could make gold but couldn't afford a new cloak.'

'Stupid?' Peter looked to heaven. 'It ought to be a crime to be as stupid as they are! There was one friar . . .' He suddenly realized that he was admitting to too much. 'Did you say that I have to tell a story? Right. I'll tell you one about an alchemist. Not MY alchemist, of course. Oh no. We never did anything *criminal*. We were research scientists, you understand. But I'll tell you about an alchemist I know of, shall I?'

So under the thin disguise of telling us a story, Peter explained just how he and his master had earned a living for the past seven years.

Fool's Gold

THE Canon – I mean this Alchemist I told you about – built his 'laboratory' in Cheapside. He heard tell that the local friar, Brother Palm, was so popular with the ladies, that they were always giving him money and presents. He never had to pay for a meal or a night's lodging and, little by little, he was becoming rather rich.

With a trembling hand, the Alchemist stitched on his humble face and stopped the friar in the street to ask for a loan. 'Just one crown,' he pleaded. 'I swear I'll return it in three days – with interest!'

'I've heard *that* before,' said Brother Palm. But because it was a public place, he was obliged to lend the money.

Three days later, at first light, the Alchemist was knocking at his door. 'I've brought back your crown. And here's another as interest.'

'Lord bless us! I never would have believed it!' said the friar, startled out of his usual cynicism. 'An honest man!'

The Alchemist's eyes widened. 'Of course, holy Brother! But I really can't begin to thank you . . . to lend money to a stranger . . . amazing! I can never repay you. You made it possible for me to complete my experiments! You must come and see!' And taking Brother Palm by the wrist, he hauled him along the streets and upstairs to a small room under the eaves of a miserable boarding house.

'Please forgive the mess,' he said, dusting off a broken stool. 'I'll be buying a manor house before the week's out.'

The smoky room was filled with enough equipment, contraptions, and chemicals to boil down London into soap. There were retorts and tubes, bowls and pipes, cylinders and balances, ladles and kilns, and little heaps of coal, sawdust and iron filings amidst bottles of every colour and substance known to man. 'My life's work!' said the Alchemist theatrically. 'And now – thanks to you – I can turn all matter to silver!'

Brother Palm's heart beat a little faster, but he was too much of a rogue himself to be entirely convinced.

'Let me show you! Let me share it with you, my great good fortune!' cried the Alchemist excitedly, lighting a fire on the table. He had Palm himself blowing on the coals to kindle them. 'Now! You add the dross, will you Brother. Anything will do!'

Brother Palm breathed in a faceful of smoke and began to cough. But he quickly gathered up a handful of wood-shavings, another of iron filings and a third of torn paper, and poured them into an earthenware jar balanced over the fire.

'Now blow, man!' urged the Alchemist. 'The fire must be hot! This is the critical stage. This is where I add *lacrima Christi* . . . a drop of *lido de jesolo* . . . and a soupçon of *vermicelli verdi* . . . in exact proportions . . . according to the secret formula.' Every bottle came down off the shelves, and drops and dribbles were added to produce clouds of smoke.

The friar puffed until his face was grisly red and he was sweating from the very sockets of his eyes.

'My dear chap! Here – wipe your face on this napkin!' said the Alchemist solicitously. And while Palm was wiping his face, the Alchemist added one more 'secret ingredient' to the jar. An ingot of silver.

The fire roared until the flames were barely visible and the jar grew so incandescent that at the merest tap, a hole opened in the base. Out ran pure silver with a small residue of iron.

The friar stared so long at it that his lids stuck to his eyeballs. 'Heaven bless your work, master scientist,' he whispered reverently. 'I never saw anything like it since the day I was born. How's it done?'

'Ah, the secret is long in the finding and precious in the keeping, Brother. I wouldn't sell it to anyone in the world unless it was you. And then it would cost you forty pounds. Do you want to see it again? You see the secret lies in the calcigination and asphixiation of the sebum while it is being catomorphized at the barometric equibriscate. The helio precipitation is extravertible.'

Again the friar stocked the jar, stoked the fire, and blew till his eyes bulged. Again the Alchemist added drops and trickles of the coloured water then, while Brother Palm wiped his face, slipped a silver ingot into the jar. Again, pure silver flowed out of the base. Why wouldn't it?

'Forty pounds, you say? A fair price for a fair gift. Teach me!'

With a flourish, the Alchemist produced a notebook. 'Everything you need to know is written in this book: the ingredients, the exact proportions, storage temperatures . . . Give me the forty pounds and I can go and buy some more chemicals while you make a few ingots yourself. Please feel free to use all the wood here – I can soon buy more . . . Shan't be long. If you have any problems, I'll help you when I get back . . .'

'Too kind . . . too kind.' Brother Palm rummaged under his habit for his fat money belt and the forty pounds. He paid small attention to the Alchemist when he counted the money, picked up the ingots and one or two other things from around the room, and went downstairs. Palm was too intent on making silver – a perpetual waterfall of silver – now that he had the formula!

With a trembling hand, Palm added the liquids in the measures described, carefully keeping his place in the notebook. He stoked and blew and poured and sealed and heated and tapped and holed and watched the earthenware jar with its cargo of sawdust and iron. A blob of pig-iron plopped on to the table. Brother Palm began again.

Six hours later, he was sitting at the top of the stairs, tear-spattered and sooty, waiting for the Alchemist to come back and tell him what he was doing wrong. He waited and waited and waited. Finally the street door banged and footsteps plodded up the stairs.

'What d'you want?' said a fierce-faced old woman. 'If you're begging, you'll get nothing from me.' Then she saw past him into the room.

'What's this? Did you do this? Who did this? What do you know about this rubbish?'

'I'm waiting for the Alchemist,' said Palm with wounded dignity.

'Who? There's nobody lives here but me. Though by the looks of it, somebody's been making free with my little home. Get off your backside, you great ape, and help me clear out all these bottles. Coal! Lord save us – who would put coal on the table!'

The friar organized a hunt. But the Alchemist was long gone – lost among the townspeople like one bad penny melting into a puddle of lead. The old lady sold all the jars and bottles for three shillings, and kept herself warm for two nights on the remaining coal.

Out of the trees burst an explosion of villagers on horseback. There was an alderman, a butcher in his apron, a woman with her skirts tucked into her belt, a vicar, a demobbed crusader, and a farmer brandishing a pitchfork. They hailed us so loudly that we could not, in all faith, ignore them.

As they caught us up, the butcher bawled, 'Have you see two riders – a fat old clergyman and a black-faced little mongrel of a boy?'

'They seem to have done you some grave offence,' said Harry.

''Sblood! When we catch 'em I'm going to hang 'em from the first tree, then quarter 'em with this cleaver. They promised to make us rich and they could no more make gold than fly in the air!'

But before Harry could speak again, the quiet Parson unexpectedly spoke up. 'I saw two riders earlier. I believe they went North, masters. God bring your hunt to a happy conclusion.'

We watched them go, the Sea Captain and the Magistrate muttering under their breaths about 'missing a good hanging'. Then Peter shook back the hood of the Monk's spare cloak and thanked him for the loan of it. The Monk, who had not noticed Peter taking it from his saddle pack, cursed loudly, and the Widow from Bath went and gave the Parson a big hug.

He blushed. 'Lord Jesus Christ is the touchstone which can turn all our deeds to gold,' he said anxiously. 'I pray He can forgive that lie of mine.'

AT the inn where we took lunch, the Summoner made a beast of himself, then bought an enormous cake, and we endured his foolery all afternoon as he pretended it was a shield and rode along with it on his arm. The Pardoner made him a wreath of hop leaves for his crown.

Most of us were too scared of the Summoner's power to fall out with him. But the begging Friar, who lived quite hand-to-mouth and could never be made to pay a fine, was free with his insults. 'I suppose you can't *help* it,' he would say pityingly. 'It's the company you keep – all those other summoners!'

But the Summoner only made pellets of cake and shied them at the Friar saying, 'Are you any better? We both play on their guilty consciences. They pay you to pray for them, and they bribe me not to report them to the bishop. What's the difference?'

'The difference is that people give freely to me. You frighten them into it – and when they've done nothing wrong, they still have to bribe you

not to *invent* sins and tell those to the bishop. Really, if you hadn't been born and raised in a pigsty, you could never crunch so hard on the bones of the poor. I heard once of a summoner who met the Devil. – Poor Devil, I say! Think of it: he has to put up with all those summoners who go to Hell when they die . . .'

'Tell us about the summoner who met the Devil,' said the Pardoner, who was nibbling on the Summoner's shield at the time.

The Summoner snatched his cake away. 'Look, whose friend are you, anyway?'

'What? Don't you want me to tell that story, then?' jeered the Friar. 'Too close to the mark, is it?'

But the Summoner pushed his loathsome face hard up against the Friar's and grinned till the cold-sore on his lip cracked. 'Do your worst, beggar, but quick! the Devil may be listening!'

Going to the Devil

WHILE he was riding out on business, a summoner once met the Devil doing just the same thing. At first he tried to make out to the Devil that he was a bailiff, knowing how people despise summoners. But the Devil knew straight off what he was. 'What are you ashamed of? You and I are in the same line of work! I carry off whatever people give me: their souls, their wives, the weeds in their garden ... You go around persuading people that if they give you five shillings you won't get them into trouble with the Bishop.' Before long, the two were swearing lifelong friendship.

'Whoever makes the most out of the day's sinners decides where we take supper,' the Devil proposed. 'Agreed?'

One thing still puzzled the Summoner. 'I know why people give me money. But why do they give their souls and so forth to you? Do you mean you disguise yourself?'

'I don't need to!' declared the Devil. 'Watch!'

106

They were just then riding past a horse and cart bogged down in a deep rut. The driver had whipped the horse to its knees and was cursing it roundly. 'Get up, you lazy beast!' The horse struggled painfully but unsuccessfully. 'Well, to the Devil with you, you mangy animal! Devil take you and the cart and everything in it! Damn you to hell!'

The Summoner gave an admiring whistle. 'I see what you mean, friend,' he whispered. 'They're yours, the cart and horse both.'

'Don't you believe it,' answered the Devil wryly. 'Wait and see.'

The horse pulled itself to its feet and, with one brave effort, dragged the cart clear. 'Ah, Bessy!' cheered the haulier. 'God and his angels bless you and send you apples every three days. I swear, you're such a lovely horse, I'll take you to heaven when I die!'

'See?' said the Devil. 'But now it's your turn.'

No sooner said than they were standing at the door of a widow-woman the Summoner had planned to visit. 'Good evening sir,' the widow said, smiling up at the Summoner.

'I've come to summon you to the Bishop to answer charges.'

The old lady crossed herself in terror. 'Mary and Joseph! What charges? I never knowingly did wrong, not in all the days of my life. Besides, I can't walk all the way to the Bishop's – not with my feet the way they are!'

The Summoner put on his best and most winning smile. 'Well look, I can see I've frightened you. It's only a *small* matter of sinfulness. I'm sure the Bishop will be merciful. Why don't you let *me* settle it for you?'

'Would you? Would you really, good Summoner?'

'Yes, yes. Give me three shillings and put your mind at rest. With three shillings in my pocket, I might even forget to tell the Bishop about your sins . . .'

'How much? I don't have three shillings in the world!' The widow's eyes narrowed as she realized what trick was afoot. 'Anyway . . . what sins exactly? No! The Devil take you and your evil blackmail – yes, and your lying tongue as well!'

The Devil poked his head round the door then, and said: 'Do you sincerely mean that, my good woman?'

'I do! May he rot in Hell for a thousand years with no time off for good behaviour. I don't know what things are coming to these days – the whole church is going to the Devil!'

'Well, well,' said the Devil, tucking the Summoner under his large and flapping cloak. 'You heard what the lady said. And since that makes me the winner, I know just where we'll take supper!'

And the Summoner, as he smelled the smell of burning, said: 'Hell.'

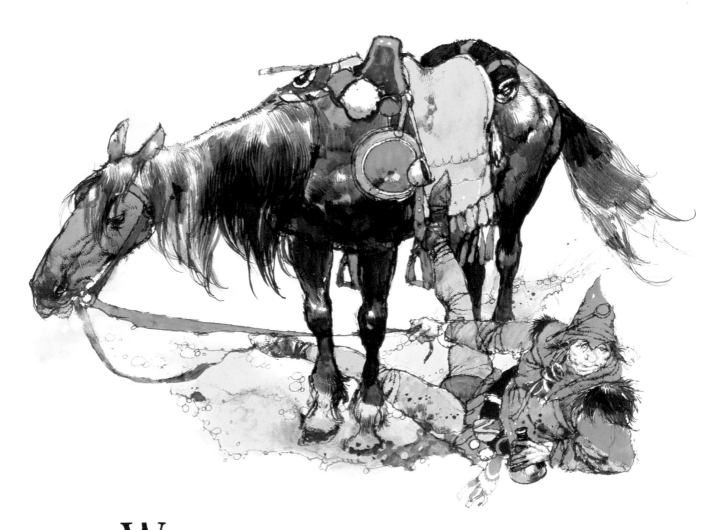

WE had the martyrdom of Saint Cecilia, and the trials of Constance (who seems to have converted half the known world to Christianity without me hearing tell of her before). The Monk then undertook to tell us the history of the world – an over-ambitious project, I thought, but it passed the time.

We were making poor progress, however, on account of the Cook's determination to fall off his horse every five minutes. We had to keep stopping to pick him up. We might just as well have poured a yard of ale into the saddle: he flowed straight out of it again. If the road had not been so muddy, I swear he would have flattened the top of his head.

To keep his mouth occupied in something other than drinking, we got him to tell us a story. But as with drinking, the Cook did not know where to stop. When almost everyone in his story had been hanged or locked up, and the Cook had fallen asleep contentedly, we were glad enough of the peace.

Kent flowed past us to right and left, bearing its flotsam: a farmhouse, a spinney, a village, a cow, a windmill, a church. Though we were fearfully weary by the end of the third day, our quarrels were still spirited and our friendships firm fixed.

'My! but this journey's done my soul good already,' said the Ploughman and there was a gentle surge of voices in agreement.

'Well of course it's done us all good,' said the Merchant. 'It's got us away from our wives!'

Since half of us were in holy orders, this did not meet with much support, and seemed to anger Harry.

'You won't complain when she's there waiting at the garden gate for you when you get home.'

'Waiting at the gate? My dear Harold, how have you lived so long and kept such a romantic notion of married life?' sneered the Merchant.

'I was widowed early,' said Harry sadly. 'And I hold it unmannerly if you are about to tell us your wife's failings without her here to defend herself.'

'Tell her faults?' The Merchant's forked beard jabbed the air like the fangs of the serpent in the Garden of Eden. 'I wouldn't dare! She might hear me. She's got better ears for eavesdropping than an owl in a tree. But I'll tell you this: I'd give the coat off my back to be a bachelor again. Do you realize? Only one merchant in six makes a profit these days, and I'm one of them. Much good it does me! My wife spends every penny!'

'You shouldn't have married such a young one,' said the Sea Captain, nodding sagely. 'That was where you went wrong.'

'Oh, that's it. That's it entirely. I always buy for value, so naturally I chose a sixteen-year-old – to give maximum wear, you understand. Worst investment I ever made.'

The Monk looked itchy and knowing. 'Sixteen, eh? You've got to be a man to handle a sixteen-year-old. Where is it you live, Master Merchant?' (I saw him make a note of the answer.)

'Proof! Proof! Take the witness box and give us your case for bachelorhood,' said Harry, doggedly sticking to the point. 'And if you can't tell us a story to prove your case, we'll call you a perjured witness!'

The Widow from Bath cast on Harry a look of undisguised admiration and, for once, said nothing at all.

I think the Merchant was a fool to tell the story he did. At the end of it everyone had a much higher regard for May than they did for January . . . But you haven't heard it yet, have you? So you don't know what I'm talking about. Judge for yourself.

Old January and Young May

ALL his life January had lived a bachelor – and right healthy, rich and cheerful he was, to prove it. But in his old age, he took it into his head to marry.

'I've missed out on a lot,' he said. And though his friends tried hard to dissuade him, his mind was made up.

He furnished his house with all the soft and breakable things women like to have about – vases, curtains, servants, cradles and the like – and built for it a garden with a high wall. Inside the garden were such delights as could only be rumoured round about, for no one but January and his bride would be allowed beyond its gate. Lastly January chose for himself a girl called May – not one day over sixteen – and married her.

Every day they would walk in the garden among the peacocks and the fountains, the hedge mazes, and the rock walls brimming with alyssum and lilies of the valley. The scents were heady, and the grass was lush under their feet. Their lips were always sticky with juice of fruits from the trees, and the dew was always wet on the hems of May's petticoats.

But January was old to be lying in wet grass, and rheumatism plagued him if he walked too long by the pools. May would have liked to be with a younger companion in the garden. In short, she would have liked to be with Damian.

Damian was a servant boy – not two days over sixteen when May came as a bride to the house. He was forever pestering her to be allowed inside the garden. And he was so young, so curly, and such fun to talk to, that she had a mind to let him see it. But how? She did not have to wait long for a solution.

In the evening of his life, January was suddenly plunged into an early night. He went stone blind.

How glad he was now that he had built the garden and taken a wife! He wagged his head at his friends, and told them: 'Where would I be now without an arm to lean on and guide me through the perfumes and sounds of my little garden, eh? Eh? . . . Where are you? Are you still there?'

Damian's chance had come. May winked an eye at him as he crept into the garden ahead of January, and supped at the fountain, and climbed a pear tree to eat its fruit. She did not see, and neither did Damian, that there were two others already in the tree.

Invisible to human eyes, the gods Pluto and Proserpine sat talking in the branches. Damian trod, unknowingly, on the god's transparent hand and he snarled inaudibly: 'You see what young people are coming to these days? Trespassing. Stealing pears. I blame the girl. She encouraged this young brat. Where's a woman's sense of *duty* to her husband nowadays?'

'Stop fretting,' said his wife, the goddess. 'Old January should never have married such a young wife. How can he give her the fun she needs? This boy here would make a much fitter husband for a sixteen-year-old.' And she ruffled Damian's hair, though he thought it was merely the breeze. Oblivious, he sat between them, eating pears. The juice ran down his chin.

'Ooo, I wish I could have one of those pears,' said May, licking her lips at the sight of Damian's pleasure.

'Pears?' said January. 'Are there pears? Oh dear, if only I could see, I'd fetch a ladder and pick one for you, my dearest.'

'That's all right, dear. If you crouch down, I can climb on to your shoulders, then you can lift me up into the branches.' And she waved to Damian.

Pluto struck his forehead. 'What are things coming to! I've a good mind to put a stop to her mischief!'

'Then I'll put a stop to yours!' said his wife.

At the very moment when Damian and May had their heads together in the tree and were eating the same pear, Pluto laid a magic finger to old January's eyes and gave him back his sight.

'Oho!' wailed the old man. 'So these are the thanks I get for marrying a young wife! My friends were right, were they? What's the meaning of it? Helping some young *boy* to steal my pears!'

For May, it was an awkward moment. It might have proved impossible if Proserpine had not whispered advice in the girl's ear.

Suddenly May clapped her hands and laughed out loud. 'Oh praise be to the gods! It worked! It worked!'

'What? What worked, you mischievious madam?' January staggered under the weight of his young wife as she sat cheering on his shoulders.

'My trick to restore your sight, of course! I went to a magician, dearest, and told him I could not bear to see you afflicted by blindness. He told me that there was no cure but for me to slap the face of a boy sitting in your own pear tree.'

Dazzled by sudden sunlight after weeks of dark, January blinked and squinted at his wife, his face screwed up in doubt.

'Don't you believe her,' whispered Pluto.

'*I didn't see you slap any boy*. All I saw was the two of you eating *my* pears in *my* pear tree. And mighty friendly you seemed about it!'

'You saw *what*?' A look of utter amazement swept May's face – and then, it seemed, a glimmer of understanding. 'I know why that was! Getting your sight back after being blind is a bit like waking up out of a deep sleep. You don't see things clearly first of all. Perhaps your eyes will only get back to normal gradually.' To Damian's great astonishment, she turned then and slapped his juice-slippery face.

'I saw it! I saw it!' declared January leaping and cavorting about under the tree, his wife clinging to his hair, her legs wrapped round his neck. 'I saw it that time, wife! My eyes are quite better. Oh, May! How can I ever thank you for getting me back my sight!'

Through the branches of the tree, Damian climbed down to the ground, bitten by the first pangs of stomach-ache, and nursing his cheek. The god Pluto put his hands on his hips disgustedly and said, 'Bah!' But then his wife caught his eye and winked and giggled and reached out to him the pear she was eating. They slipped away, hand in invisible hand.

'Be careful, my love,' said May as she slithered off her husband's shoulders. 'The magician did tell me to warn you – your eyesight may come and go for the first weeks. Or rather you may *think* you see the most extraordinary things when you don't at all. You will be patient, won't you?'

'Oh, yes, yes, my dear! For instance, I *think* I see you even now arm-in-arm with the same boy, and you're stroking his cheek. But I know it's just my eyes playing tricks on me . . .'

'Yes, dear, just your eyes,' said May.

'And good luck to her, I say,' said the Widow-in-the-Hat. 'I like everybody to be happy at the end of a story. That's the most important thing.'

The Merchant snarled bitterly. 'It's only in stories that people end up happy.'

The Sea Captain put an arm round his shoulders and pointed towards the horizon. 'Well that's today's happy ending. One day at a time, eh old friend?'

We all looked in the direction the Captain was pointing. Every detail of the countryside had been blotted out by dusk, and the sky was as dark as gabardine. But two or three miles away, rising out of the gloom like the mast of a foundering ship, was the spire of Canterbury.

Our horses' ears, like little church spires themselves, pricked towards the cathedral. 'They can smell their dinner,' said the Prioress Eglantine, patting her stomach.

'Perhaps,' said Brother John, patting his horse.

Epilogue

W<small>E</small> made good time along the Rheims Way and into Canterbury, clattering through a gate in the wall so narrow that I feared for the Widow's hat. After the mud and turf of the country ride, the cobblestones jarred through the horses' stiffening legs. We were glad to tumble off outside the Templar's Hospital.

'I'd prefer to spend the night at an inn,' said the Miller. But, as it was, our party was so big that it took every bed the friars could offer us. No inn in Canterbury would have been big enough.

Ranged along the refectory table, we shifted uncomfortably on our benches after the long ride, and were too tired to speak. Only as we wiped the trenchers clean with crusts of bread, and supped a second cup of wine, did we begin to feel talkative again.

'Well?' said the Summoner leaning across to rap the table in front of Harry. 'Who won?'

'Ah,' said Harry. 'Is that everybody, then? No more stories?'

We looked at each other, trying to match each face to the story it had told. 'Well, it's obvious, isn't it?' said the Miller. 'For a laugh it's got to be the Friar, devil take him. That's all supposing I can't vote for myself.' His flaring nostrils so terrified the Haberdasher that he immediately voted for Matt.

'Humorous stories are all very well,' said the Prioress, licking her lips so that no crumb should escape, 'but we must consider the VALUE of the stories. How much did they teach us about LIFE?'

'Hear, hear!' squeaked the Summoner, plastering his hair across his skull with the palm of a sweaty hand.

I voted for Brother John's story myself. But then I've always liked words over and above the meaning wrapped up in them.

The Knight and his son both thought it merest chivalry to vote for a lady. They gave one look at the Widow, and voted for the young nun. But when the Scholar was pressed for an opinion, he said, 'Um, I'm afraid I wasn't listening very much. Sorry.'

'Where does that leave us?' snapped the Magistrate waspishly.

To my astonishment, I noticed that Harry was holding hands under the table with the Widow. 'What did you say?' he asked when he noticed that everyone's eyes were on him.

'It's a split vote,' I explained. 'We can't agree who won.'

'Oh, I can tell you that,' Harry said, and his florid face split into a smile as broad and white as a harvest moon. 'I won.'

There were murmurs of discontent. Had the contest been rigged from the start? Was the referee about to change the rules in his own favour? 'I have won the agreement of this excellent lady,' said Harry, standing up and bowing to the Widow, 'to become my wife. You're all invited to the wedding when we get back to Southwark.'

The Prioress sniffed. The Pardoner gave a disapproving bleat. But most of us cheered and stamped and banged our mugs on the table. 'But whose story was *best*?' insisted the Magistrate peevishly.

The Widow got to her feet, as majestic as an oak tree. She patted Harry on his bald head. 'Your word is absolutely final, of course, my pet,' she said, 'but if I could venture a suggestion . . . These people won't be content till someone is declared Best Storyteller. Now there's not one story with more votes than another. So I suggest that we all tell another story on the way back – to part the sheep from the goats, so to speak.'

I tell you, reader, you never saw an idea so well received.

'I'll tell you about the time I fought smugglers in the Spanish Main,' said the Ship's Captain.

'Have you heard the one about the three-legged ox?' asked the Miller.

116

'There's the sweetest little story I once heard about a martyred virgin who was boiled to death in . . .'

'Wait till you hear mine, though!'

'Stop!'

The Parson was holding up his hand for silence. 'Let there be stories for every mile of the way home. But let us give over tomorrow to the Truth. The truth is that the blessed Thomas à Becket, not a stone's throw from this very spot, laid down his life for the love of God. He brought us here, and tomorrow it's him we'll pray to in the Cathedral. That's the Truth. That's no story. That's all I wanted to say.' And he sat down.

He had silenced us. I sat thinking about poor Saint Thomas lying on the cold stone floor with his murderers' swords sharp at his forehead – and all our enjoyment suddenly seemed a terrible, callous, frivolous thing.

'So,' Brother John said, not in the least cast down. 'Let's take ourselves and our thanksgiving to the good man's shrine. Then maybe all the saints in heaven will look down on our homeward journey and listen in on our stories. I daresay they relish a good story as much as the next man.'

'Amen,' said the Parson thoughtfully.

'Amen!' roared the rest of us.

All except the Cook, who was asleep under the table.

For
Daphne and Jadwiga

The publishers are grateful to Ron Ullyatt for his
encouragement in the preparation of this book.

OXFORD
UNIVERSITY PRESS
Great Clarendon Street, Oxford OX2 6DP

Oxford New York
Athens Auckland Bangkok Bogotá Buenos Aires Calcutta Cape Town
Chennai Dar es Salaam Delhi Florence Hong Kong Istanbul Karachi
Kuala Lumpur Madrid Melbourne Mexico City Mumbai Nairobi
Paris São Paulo Singapore Taipei Tokyo Toronto Warsaw

and associated companies in
Berlin Ibadan

Oxford is a trade mark of Oxford University Press

© Geraldine McCaughrean 1984
Illustrations © Victor Ambrus 1984

First published 1984
Reprinted 1991, (Re-issue) 1995
First published in paperback 1988
Reprinted 1991, 1993, 1995, 1997
Reissued in paperback 1999
Reprinted 1999

British Library Cataloguing in Publication Data

McCaughrean, Geraldine
The Canterbury Tales
I. Title   II. Ambrus, Victor   III. Chaucer,
Geoffrey
823' .914[J]   PZ7

ISBN 0–19–278109–X (Hardback)
ISBN 0–19–274181–0 (Paperback)

Typeset by Wyvern Typesetting Ltd, Bristol
Printed in Hong Kong